I0761565

RED GHOST
WHITE GHOST

RED GHOST
WHITE GHOST

stories and essays by Kita Morio

TRANSLATED WITH AN INTRODUCTION BY

MASAKO INAMOTO

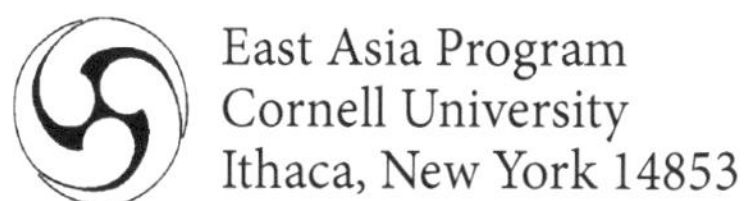

East Asia Program
Cornell University
Ithaca, New York 14853

The Cornell East Asia Series is published by the Cornell University East Asia Program (distinct from Cornell University Press). We publish books on a variety of scholarly topics relating to East Asia as a service to the academic community and the general public. Standing Orders, which provide for automatic notification and invoicing of each title in the series upon publication, are accepted. Address submission inquiries to CEAS Editorial Board, East Asia Program, Cornell University, 140 Uris Hall, Ithaca New York 14853-7601.

Cover credit: Reproduced with permission. *Chikyū o hanareta obake*
(地球を離れたお化け The ghosts that left Earth)
Cover design: Mai

Number 188 in the Cornell East Asia Series.
New Japanese Horizon Series Editors:
Michiko Wilson/Gustav Heldt/Doug Merwin

ISSN: 1050-2955
ISBN: 978-1-939161-68-0 hardcover
ISBN: 978-1-939161-88-8 paperback
E-book: 978-1-942242-88-8 e-book
Library of Congress Control Number: 2018957153

♾ The paper in this book meets the requirements for permanence of ISO 9706:1994.

These translations are
for my mother and the memory of my father

contents

acknowledgments

I wish to express my sincere appreciation to Saitō Kimiko who graciously granted permission to translate these stories and essays, to use the painting *Chikyū o hanareta obake* (The ghosts that left Earth) by Kita Morio for the cover, and to include Kita's photo in this book; to Endō Masahiro, Director of the Gen Foundation in Yamagata, Japan, who so kindly sent me the digital images of the painting and the photo; and to Shiotani Mamiko at the Japan Foreign-Rights Centre who contacted Mrs. Saitō numerous times on my behalf.

I am very grateful to Professor Richard Torrance, Margaret Pearson, and Sue Rosenberg for reading portions of the early drafts and offering their suggestions, and to Mary-Beth O'Brien for the helpful information on the writer Thomas Mann and his work *Tonio Kröger.* When it came time to revise the draft, Mike Mudrovic and Dylan Ellefson helped me greatly, for which I am truly thankful. Very special thanks to Josh D'Andrea who assisted me at the very final stage of the revision. I would also like to express my appreciation to the anonymous readers for their valuable comments.

I am truly grateful to the editors of the New Japanese Horizons Series for selecting my manuscript, and especially to Professor Michiko Wilson for her continuous guidance. I would also like to express my sincere gratitude to Mai Shaikhanuar-Cota, Managing Editor at the Cornell East Asia Series, who could not have been more generous with her help, support, and patience from the beginning to the end of this project. A Skidmore College Faculty Development Grant partially funded the publication of this book, for which I am grateful.

Warmest thanks to the friends and colleagues who have helped and encouraged me throughout the various stages of the project. I am confident they know who they are so I will omit a lengthy list of names here, but I am truly thankful for them all.

I am grateful to my family, especially my mother, Kiyo, my brother, Hiroshi, and my husband, Robert Longhurst, for their unfailing support.

note on names

Names of Japanese persons are given in the traditional order, surnames first. When using one-name references to authors, I follow customary usage: for example, Kita for Kita Morio, but Mokichi for Saitō Mokichi.

A foghorn sounded from far away, and then, unexpectedly close by, another erupted like an ancient mythological giant groaning. In fact, there was no better word than "erupt" to describe the way the foghorn blasted. The eruption of that foghorn blast disappeared into the many layers of dense fog, and the next thing I heard was someone striking a bell. Evidently a ship was sailing in this dense fog, and suddenly foghorns and bells were sounding everywhere, signaling each other to indicate their locations. The sounds echoed heavily, as if from the far corners of the earth, and because the bells were so faint, they seemed even more melancholy.

—"At the Mouth of the River"

Kita Morio, "Kakō nite" 河口にて, in *Kita Morio zenshū* 北杜夫全集 (Tokyo: Shinchōsha, 1977), 2:224. All translations from the Japanese are mine unless otherwise noted. Hereafter, Kita Morio, *Kita Morio zenshū*, 15 vols. (Tokyo: Shinchōsha, 1976–1977) is referred to in the notes as *KMZ*.

From time to time we rang our bells as if to confirm each other's continued presence. The freighter was equipped with a fine big bell at the bow, but at the stern someone clanged on what might have been a large frying pan. This instrument had been selected after considerable experimentation with oil drums and God knows what else. … A deep basso foghorn would suddenly assault our ears, and croaks, toots, and honks would respond from every direction. The horn of the freighter next to us sounded like a serious case of whooping cough.

—*Doctor Manbō at Sea*

Kita Morio, *Doctor Manbō at Sea*, trans. Ralph McCarthy (Tokyo: Kōdansha International, 1987), 185.

introduction

On October 26, 2011, the Japanese media reported that one of the most prolific, versatile, and beloved postwar writers in Japan, Kita Morio (b. 1927), had passed away two days earlier, on October 24. The following day, Kita was the subject of front-page morning columns in the four leading national daily newspapers.[1] One columnist wrote that Kita was a versatile writer, another said that he had skillfully written in two totally different modes: his serious work, suffused with lyricism, and his comical Doctor Manbō series. A third columnist noted that Kita had produced a wide range of work from long serious novels to comical essays, fantasy novels, and children's stories.[2] Indeed, his writing styles are so varied that literary scholars have said that "[a] literary schizophrenia is evident in his work."[3] The epigraphs above from "At the Mouth of the River" and *Doctor Manbō at Sea*, which depict the same scene but in different styles, exemplify the "schizophrenic" dichotomy between the serious and the comic that characterizes Kita's writing.

Kita Morio, also known by his literary persona Dokutoru Manbō (Doctor Manbō, which means "Doctor Sunfish"), became well known in Japan as a writer following the publication of two of his works in 1960: *Dokutoru Manbō kōkaiki* どくとるマンボウ航海記

1. The four newspapers were the *Asahi*, *Mainichi*, *Nihon Keizai*, and *Yomiuri Shinbun*.
2. See "Tensei jingo" 天声人語, *Asahi Shinbun*, October 27, 2011; "Shunjū" 春秋, *Nihon Keizai Shinbun*, October 27, 2011; and "Yoroku" 余禄, *Mainichi Shinbun*, October 27, 2011.
3. J. Thomas Rimer and Van C. Gessel, eds., *The Columbia Anthology of Modern Japanese Literature* (New York: Columbia University Press, 2007), 2:170.

(Doctor Manbō at sea) in March and *Yoru to kiri no sumi de* 夜と霧の隅で (In the corner of night and fog) in May.[4] The two works are written in completely different styles. The former is one of the very first overseas travelogues in postwar Japan and it served as a vehicle for Kita to record, in a most comical manner, his alter ego's journey as a ship's doctor.[5] The latter is a somber novel that depicts the attempts of German psychiatrists to save their mental patients from the Nazis. The former became a bestseller immediately after it was published, while the latter received the Akutagawa Prize, the most prestigious literary award for a serious work of fiction by a new or rising writer in Japan.

When *Yoru to kiri no sumi de* received the Akutagawa Prize, *Dokutoru Manbō kōkaiki* was already selling extremely well. Therefore, some literary critics thought that Kita might become the first writer in the history of Japanese literature to be simultaneously awarded the Akutagawa Prize and the Naoki Prize, which is given to a writer of popular literature.[6] Kita did not win the Naoki Prize, but the success of both works immediately made him known as a writer who was able to write in very different literary modes. In fact, some literary critics were surprised to realize that the two works, written in such different styles, were produced by the same author.[7] After 1960, Kita continued to write both serious and humorous works simultaneously, attracting large readerships that can be divided into two groups: *Manbō-ha* (Manbō group) and *Yūrei-ha* (Ghost group). Readers in the Manbō group favor Kita's comical works, which are often written with a title that begins with Doctor Manbō or Manbō;[8] while readers in the Ghost

---

4. The direct translation of *Dokutoru Manbō kōkaiki* is "The voyage of Doctor Manbō." However, because Ralph McCarthy has already translated the work into English under the title *Doctor Manbo at Sea*, I use the same title here except that I changed *Manbo* to *Manbō* for the sake of consistency.
5. It should be noted that, although the work is written based on a voyage he took, it is still a fictional account.
6. Okuno Takeo, "Tanpen ni tsuite" 短編について, *Kita Morio no bungaku sekai* 北杜夫の文学世界 (Tokyo: Chūō Kōronsha, 1978), 109.
7. "Shijō to yūmoa jizai: sakka Kita Morio san shikyo" 詩情とユーモア自在 作家·北杜夫さん死去, *Asahi Shinbun* (evening edition), October 26, 2011, 11.
8. If the title of a book begins with "Doctor Manbō," the book has a consistent theme. On the other hand, if the title begins with simply "Manbō," the work is a

group prefer lyrical, serious fiction such as *Yūrei* 幽霊 (Ghosts, 1953–1954), Kita's first published novel.

Critics agree that Kita was one of Japan's most popular writers of his time.[9] However, despite this popularity and the high quality of his works, he has received little attention from literary scholars. Many critics have speculated that this is because of his comical works. Nada Inada, a writer, literary critic, and psychiatrist, pointedly argues that Kita's works have not received their due attention because literary criticism in Japan has been focused only on serious, ideological literature, which has excluded other styles such as comical works and science fiction.[10] Pointing out that no less a writer than Mishima Yukio valued Kita's serious literature but despised his comical works, the literary scholar Yamada Hiromitsu argues that the latter have prevented Kita from receiving the scholarly attention he deserves.[11] Their speculations seem valid. Indeed, there is a notable lack of humor in acclaimed works of modern Japanese literature, while the generally marginalized status of comical writing has generated lively discussions among literary scholars.

---

collection of pieces of writing with no consistent theme. See Kita Morio, "Sōsaku yowa" 創作余話 in *Kita Morio zenshū geppō* 北杜夫全集月報, no. 15:1, in vol. 15 of *KMZ* (1977). *Geppō* (Monthly Report) is supplemented to each volume of *Kita Morio zenshū*.

9. For example, Yamada Hiromitsu argues that Kita was the most popular writer in the contemporary period. Akiyama Shun and Nada Inada also maintain that Kita was, along with Ōe Kenzaburō, the most loved writer (at the time), who had a wide readership. See Yamada Hiromitsu, "Kita Morio" 北杜夫 (Kita Morio), in *Shin kenkyū shiryō gendai Nihon bungaku* 新研究資料現代日本文学, ed. Asai Kiyoshi, et al. (Tokyo: Meiji Shoin, 2000) 2:166; Akiyama Shun, "'*Yūrei*' to '*Manbō*' no tairitsu" 「幽霊」と「マンボウ」の対立, *Kita Morio no sekai* 北杜夫の世界 (Tokyo: Shinpyōsha, 1979), 139; and Nada Inada, "Kaisetsu" 解説, in *Kita Morio shīu* 北杜夫集, vol. 61 of *Shinchō Nihon bungaku* 新潮日本文学 (Tokyo: Shinchōsha, 1968), 696, respectively. Newspaper columnists also wrote that Kita was a "tremendously popular" novelist and "*jidai no chōji* 時代の寵児 (a favorite [novelist)] of the time)." See "Yūmoa tsuranuita isshō" ユーモア貫いた一生, *Yomiuri Shinbun* (evening edition), October 26, 2011, and "Yūmoa eien ni" ユーモア永遠に, *Mainichi Shinbun* (evening edition), October 26, 2011, respectively.

10. See Nada Inada, "Kaisetsu," 700.

11. Yamada, "Kita Morio," 166.

Comical Writing in Japanese Literature

Although comical writing has been regarded as "inferior" in modern Japanese literary circles, works of humor in premodern Japanese literature have been celebrated by modern intellectuals. In his essay "Gesakusha no dentō" 戯作者の伝統 (The tradition of playful writers), the folklorist Yanagita Kunio pointed out the existence of comical expressions in the *Kojiki* 古事記 (Records of ancient matters, 712), the oldest extant chronicle in Japan, and asserted that Japanese people have been fond of laughter since ancient times.[12] The Heian period (794–1185) masterpiece, Murasaki Shikibu's *Genji monogatari* 源氏物語 (The tale of Genji), contains comic relief in episodes such as the red-nosed Suetsumuhana (Safflower Princess) and Gen no Naishi no Suke (Naishi), an elderly lady who tries to seduce Prince Genji. In *Makura no sōshi* 枕草子 (The pillow book), another literary classic of the Heian period, the author Sei Shōnagon recorded a detailed account of Japanese court life. Some of her candid opinions about people, things, and the witty conversations among the court ladies are comical.

In medieval literature, comical tales appear in *Konjaku monogatari shū* 今昔物語集 (Tales of times now past) compiled in the late Heian period, and in *Uji shūi monogatari* 宇治拾遺物語 (Tales from the later gleanings of Uji) from the Kamakura period (1185–1333). *Kyōgen*, a drama form based on comic dialogue, was developed in conjunction with the more serious and sedate Noh theater in the Muromachi period (1333–1573). With the rise of the culture of urban commoners (*chōnin bunka*) in the Edo period (1600–1868), satirical and comical works flourished in a variety of literary genres. *Senryū* (a short poetic form similar to *Haiku*), *kyōka* (comic verse form), and *gesaku* (playful fiction) are just a few examples of comical or humorous genres in premodern Japanese literature. In his three-volume work *Nihon no yūmoa* (Japanese humor), Oda Shōkichi, an essayist and broadcast writer, examined humorous, comical, and satirical ele-

12. Yanagita Kunio, "Gesakusha no dentō" 戯作者の伝統, in *Teihon Yanagita Kunio shū* 定本柳田国男集 (Tokyo: Chikuma Shobō, 1972), 7:187.

ments in various premodern literary works. He claimed that "Japanese literature began its history as a literature of the '*okashi*' (charming/amusing)."[13] In light of this history, we question how humorous and comical writing have come to be relegated to the sidelines of mainstream literature in modern Japan.

In the first chapter of his book *Studies of Comic Spirits in Modern Japanese Literature*, Joel R. Cohn provides an overview of the comic tradition in Japanese literature and examines the disappearance of comic spirits in modern Japanese literature. According to Cohn, even though the nation transitioned to the "modern" era in the beginning of the Meiji period (1868–1912), the Neo-Confucian values embraced by the Tokugawa Shogunate were still held by the Meiji elites, who considered literature as a means to provide moral or spiritual education. Under the circumstances, only seriousness was valued, and comical, playful *gesaku*, which flourished in the late Edo period, was considered nothing but frivolous "anti-literature."[14] As time progressed, Neo-Confucian ideas gradually diminished in influence. However, the new elites, who had been educated in the new school system and felt they carried the heavy responsibility of modernizing the nation to catch up with Western countries, continued to honor seriousness and disdain frivolity in literature.

This is not to say that there were no comical works produced in the Meiji or the Taishō (1912–1926) periods. Natsume Sōseki's earlier works, *Wagahai wa neko de aru* 我輩は猫である (I am a cat, 1905–1906) and *Botchan* 坊っちゃん (Young master, 1906), are known as comical and satirical novels. However, as Cohn points out, Sōseki gradually moved away from comedy to darker psychological novels, and while he was making the transition, Tayama Katai's *Futon* 蒲団

13. Oda Shōkichi, "Warau mono to warawareru mono" 笑う者と笑われる者, in *Koten, Setsuwa hen* 古典·説話篇, vol. 2 of *Nihon no yūmoa* 日本のユーモア (Tokyo: Chikuma Shobō, 1987), 415.

14. Joel R. Cohn, *Studies in the Comic Spirits in Modern Japanese Fiction* (Cambridge: Harvard University Asia Center, 1998), 20. Edward Fowler also states that vulgar, frivolous fiction and serious, refined nonfiction literature were considered totally different things in the Edo period, and that this idea continued into the Meiji period. See Edward Fowler, *The Rhetoric of Confession: Shishōsetsu in Early Twentieth-Century Japanese Fiction* (Berkeley: University of California Press, 1988), 23.

(The quilt) was published in 1907. *Futon* has been widely considered the first *shishōsetsu*, and its publication is believed to be the beginning of the dominance, which lasted for the next two decades, of *shishōsetsu* in the Japanese literary world.[15] *Shishōsetsu*, often described as autobiographical fiction or confessional literature, grew out of the Japanese naturalist movement called *shizenshugi*, and it was believed that the *shishōsetsu* writers were writing down their own personal experiences in their works.[16] The ultimate goal of *shizenshugi* writers, including *shishōsetsu* writers, was to depict things sincerely and "with a minimum of authorial fabrication and elaboration."[17] Therefore, writing *shishōsetsu* meant that writers exposed even the dark, shameful side of their lives with absolute honesty, in the manner of a confession.[18] When being totally "sincere," "truthful," and "honest" were absolute ideals, there was no room for humor. Cohn considers the dominance of *shizenshugi*, especially its progeny *shishōsetsu*, in the Japanese literary world as the "gravest" of circumstances for the development of comic fiction in Japan.[19] Literary critic Nakamura Mitsuo also blamed the Meiji and Taishō *shizenshugi* writers for eliminating humor as an important literary element. He argued that these writers failed to see humorous elements and saw only serious, somber aspects

---

15. Edward Fowler states that "the *shishōsetsu* so dominated the Taishō literary world that the phrase 'Taishō literature' (*Taishō bungaku*) now connotes its heyday." Fowler, 128.
16. Sharalyn Orbaugh, "Naturalism and the Emergence of the *Shishōsetsu* (Personal Novel)," in *The Columbia Companion to Modern East Asian Literature*, ed. Joshua S. Mostow, Kirk A. Denton, Bruce Fulton, and Sharalyn Orbaugh (New York: Columbia University Press, 2003), 138.
17. William Tyler, "Part One: Anti-Naturalism," *Modanizumu: Modernist Fiction from Japan 1913-1938*, ed. William Tyler (Honolulu: University of Hawai'i Press, 2008), 56.
18. It should be noted that, although many works that are considered *shishōsetsu* are based on the writers' lives, the examination of the works suggests that they are not totally nonfiction. See Fowler, xix; and Sharalyn Orbaugh, 138. For a thorough examination of *shishōsetsu*, see Edward Fowler, *The Rhetoric of Confession: Shishōsetsu in Early Twentieth-Century Japanese Fiction* (Berkeley: University of California Press, 1988); Irmela Hijiya-Kirschmerit, *Rituals of Self-Revelation: Shishōsetsu as Literary Genre and Socio-Cultural Phenomenon* (Cambridge: Harvard University Press, 1996); and Tomi Suzuki, *Narrating the Self: Fictions of Japanese Modernity* (Stanford: Stanford University Press, 1996).
19. Cohn, *Studies in the Comic Spirits*, 24.

in the Western works that were the models for their own texts, and he called this "the worst mistake" that the *shizenshugi* writers made.[20]

Although *shizenshugi* flourished only briefly, Cohn claims that "in Japanese high culture, the cult of seriousness … has persistently retained such formidable power and prestige that comic artists have had a great deal of trouble presenting their work as a legitimate alternative."[21] It was under precisely these conditions that Kita Morio became well known as the author of the comical travelogue *Dokutoru Manbō kōkaiki*. Kita was fully aware of the "cult of seriousness" in Japanese literary circles and tried to restore a marginalized comic tradition to its rightful place in modern Japanese literature.[22] He continued to write stories and essays filled with comic spirit while producing serious novels and novellas at the same time.

In addition to *Yoru to kiri no sumi de*, Kita's successful works in the serious genre include *Nireke no hitobito* 楡家の人びと (The House of Nire, 1964); *Shiroki taoyaka na mine* 白きたおやかな峰 (White Graceful Peak, 1966), which was written based on his own experience of participating in a Diran Peak expedition as the team doctor; *Kagayakeru aoki sora no shita de* 輝ける碧き空の下で (Beneath the shining azure sky, Part One in 1982 and Part Two in 1986), a literary account of the Japanese immigrants in Brazil; and his critical biography of his father, Saitō Mokichi. This biography consists of four volumes: *Seinen Mokichi* 青年茂吉 (Mokichi in youth, 1991), *Sōnen Mokichi* 壮年茂吉 (Mokichi in the prime of life, 1993), *Mokichi hōkō* 茂吉彷徨 (Wandering Mokichi, 1996), and *Mokichi ban'nen* 茂吉晩年 (Mokichi in his last years, 1998). Kita won several of Japan's acclaimed literary prizes, including the aforementioned Akutagawa Prize, the

---

20. Nakamura Mitsuo, "Warai no sōshitsu" 笑いの喪失, in *Nakamura Mitsuo zenshū* 中村光男全集 (Tokyo: Chikuma Shobō, 1972), 10:109.
21. Cohn, *Studies in the Comic Spirits,* l.
22. Kita claimed that he had revived spontaneous, exaggerated humor of Edo literature in his work. See Kita, *Manbō yuigonjō* マンボウ遺言状 (Tokyo, Shinchōsha, 2001), 57. Some critics have compared Kita's humor to that of Natsume Sōseki or of the Edo Period. See, for example, Hasegawa Izumi, *Sengo bungakushi* 戦後文学史 (Tokyo: Meiji Shoin, 1974), 61; Hara Shirō and Mori Reiko, "Kita Morio to 'Bungei Shuto'" 北杜夫と『文芸首都』, in *Kita Morio no sekai* 北杜夫の世界 (Tokyo: Shinpyōsha, 1979), 133.

Mainichi Publication Culture Award for *Nireke no hitobito*, the Japan Literary Prize for *Kagayakeru aoki sora no shita de*, and the Osaragi Jirō Prize for the biography of Saitō Mokichi.

The next section provides a brief biographical overview of Kita Morio's life, as the information offers some important background to his works.

Kita Morio's Life and Work

Kita Morio was born Saitō Sōkichi in Aoyama, Tokyo, on May 1, 1927, the third child of Saitō Mokichi, a prominent *tanka* poet, and his wife, Teruko. When Kita was born, Mokichi was forty-four, already a very well-known poet in the Araragi school, a psychiatrist, and also director of the Aoyama Mental Hospital founded by his father-in-law, Saitō Kiichi.[23] Aoyama, with its famous designer boutiques and upscale restaurants, is known today as one of the wealthiest neighborhoods in Tokyo. However, when Kita was a child, there were many open fields where neighborhood children gathered to play. There were also two cemeteries in his neighborhood: Aoyama Cemetery, Japan's first municipal cemetery, and its Tateyama branch. Kita said that open fields and cemeteries were landscapes that became engraved in his heart (*gen fūkei* 原風景)[24]—he often wrote about ghosts and open fields in his novels, stories, and essays.

Kita's parents, Mokichi and Teruko, did not get along as husband and wife. Their personalities were very different, like "water and oil" or "one extreme and the other extreme."[25] Mokichi had grown up in a small farming village in northern Japan and had led a simple life.

23. Saitō Mokichi was adopted by Saitō Kiichi as a husband for Kiichi's second daughter, Teruko, in 1905, and Mokichi and Teruko got married in 1914. Saitō Kiichi was a self-made, popular, and successful medical doctor. He also served as a member of the Japanese Diet from 1917 to 1920.

24. Kita, "Yukiyama de tōshi" 雪山で凍死, *Bungei Shunjū* 文藝春秋 (January 2005): 311.

25. Kita, *Seinen Mokichi* 青年茂吉 (Tokyo: Iwanami Shoten, 2001), 44. Saitō Shigeta, Kita's older brother who was a psychiatrist and essayist also wrote that his par-

Teruko was the daughter of a bourgeois family and her father was a successful psychiatrist in Tokyo. She had studied at Gakushūin, where half of her classmates were members of noble families. She had expensive tastes, and was strong-minded and free-willed.[26] In 1933, when Kita was six years old, the newspaper reported on the so-called Dance Hall Affair (*Dansu hōru jiken*): a popular male dancer had been arrested because of his relationships with his patrons who included wealthy women, one of whom was Teruko. While the newspaper did not reveal Teruko's name, it referred to her as "the wife of the director of a hospital."[27] Both Mokichi and Teruko were questioned by the police. Enraged, Mokichi ordered Teruko to leave the house and did not allow her to return until 1945. Even though Kita and his siblings were visiting her regularly a year later, it is not difficult to imagine what a devastating experience it must have been for the six-year old boy to be suddenly separated from his mother. In two of his serious novels that have strong autobiographical roots, *Yūrei* and *Nireke no hitobito*, the disappearance of the mother is depicted, although the scandal in which Teruko was involved is not mentioned in either of the works.

In the fourth grade, Kita began collecting insects as his summer vacation project, and this eventually led him to join a natural science club when he entered Azabu Middle School. His enthusiasm for insects lasted throughout his life.[28] During the Great Yamanote Air Raid on May 25, 1945, Kita's house in Aoyama burned down and his family

ents' marriage was "fundamentally impossible" and was "out of balance." Saitō Shigeta, *Mokichi no taishū* 茂吉の体臭 (Tokyo: Iwanami Shoten, 2000), 208.

26. Kita, "Nezu yama" 根津山, in *Haha no kage* 母の影 (Tokyo: Shinchōsha, 1994), 28–29.

27. "Yūkan madamu 'dansu hōru jiken' to bundanjin tobaku issei kenkyo" 有閑マダム「ダンスホール事件」と文壇人賭博一斉検挙, *Shinchō* 新潮 (July 2005): 68–69.

28. He exhibited his rich knowledge of insects in *Dokutoru Manbō konchūki* どくとるマンボウ昆虫記 (Doctor Manbō's book of insects, 1961). A newly discovered species of beetle was named after Kita in 2011: its scientific name is *"eumaladera kitamorioi,"* and its Japanese name is *"Manbō birōdo kogane"* (Manbō velvet beetle). The person who discovered the beetle was one of the passionate readers of *Doctor Manbō's Book of Insects* so he named the beetle after Kita to honor him.

took shelter in the house of a relative. Kita left Tokyo to attend Matsumoto High School in Nagano Prefecture shortly after.[29]

When Kita left for Matsumoto, a relative presented him with an anthology written by Mokichi. Kita had never read his father's poems until then, but when he began reading the anthology in the train on the way to Matsumoto, he became captivated and was deeply moved by the poems. Mokichi had a bad temper and Kita and his siblings were afraid of him, but from this time forward, Kita came to respect his father as a truly exceptional poet. In several of his essays, Kita humorously recorded the ambivalent feelings he had toward his father: as an exceptional poet whom he highly respected, and as an irritable, scary, and stubborn father.

Kita was interested in science and hardly ever read serious literary works before entering high school. In time, influenced by his professors and upper classmen at school, he began reading works by Western and Eastern philosophers and writers. These works, especially those of Thomas Mann, would become Kita's favorites in his university years.[30]

When it came time to decide what course to take after graduating from high school, Kita desired to become an entomologist. However, he met with fierce opposition from Mokichi, who expected Kita to become a medical doctor like himself. Kita thus gave up studying zoology and decided, or was rather compelled, to go into medicine and entered Tōhoku University School of Medicine in Sendai, Miyagi Prefecture, in 1948. However, Kita soon began to feel uneasy about committing his life to medicine. He had become totally fascinated by Thomas Mann's works by then, especially the novella *Tonio Kröger*, which depicts a man's life from his schoolboy days to his adulthood. The protagonist, Tonio Kröger, later becomes a famous novelist but

---

29. Kita went to Matsumoto High School (present-day Shinshū University) under the prewar school system in Japan. The school's name is sometimes translated as Matsumoto Higher School, but because the term "higher school" is not commonly used in English, I have translated it as Matsumoto High School.
30. Kita's *Dokutoru Manbō seishunki* どくとるマンボウ青春記 (Doctor Manbō's book of youth) is based on his experiences at Matsumoto High School and Tōhoku University. It is one of his most popular works in the Manbō series.

struggles to reconcile the conflicting qualities inherited, on the one hand, from his father, a northern German bourgeois merchant, and, on the other, from his mother, who was from the south and was artistically inclined. Kita repeatedly read the story and began to think that, just like Tonio, he was cursed and destined to write literature.[31] In a way, Kita indeed resembled Tonio Kröger because his parents were very different from each other and Kita also struggled about art and what he was expected to do.

While still studying at the university, Kita began sending his poems and short stories to literary magazines and joined *Bungei Shuto*, a literary group in Tokyo. However, being the son of Mokichi, arguably the most successful *tanka* poet in modern Japan, put significant pressure on Kita, who was afraid of shaming his father by writing mediocre stories. In order to hide his identity as Mokichi's son, he wrote under the pseudonym Kita Morio. Kita's earlier works are filled with lyricism and contain no comical elements; but his playfulness, which would later become manifest in many of his essays, was already apparent in how he chose his pseudonym: the last name Kita, which means "north" in Japanese, was chosen because he was living in colder regions such as Matsumoto and Sendai. For his first name, in the beginning he had planned to use 杜二夫, which is read as "Toni-o," taken from Tonio Kröger. However, realizing that Tonio would sound strange as a Japanese writer's pseudonym, he removed the middle character 二 and made it 杜夫, which reads as "Morio."[32] According to Kita, his original plan for his last name was to use the characters "north," "south," "east," and "west," respectively.[33]

---

31. Kita, "Gōman to tōkai" 傲慢と韜晦, in *Sono Ayako, Kita Morio* 曽野綾子·北杜夫, by Sono Ayako and Kita Morio, 474, vol. 16 of *De Luxe warera no bungaku* De Luxe われらの文学 (Tokyo: Kōdansha, 1969).

32. Kita, *Dokutoru Manbō seishunki,* 214.

33. There may be more to the reason why he chose *kita* (north) as the last name of his pseudonym. As mentioned earlier, there is an essential dichotomy in *Tonio Kröger*: the north, represented by the bourgeois father's legacy as a Kröger, and the south, epitomized by the name Antonio inherited from his mother, who is from the south. Therefore, his original pseudonym, Kita Tonio, could signify Tonio Kröger (in the Western name order). Although Kita did not mention this in any of his essays, as an avid reader of *Tonio Kröger*, he must have been aware of the dichotomy.

In March 1952, Kita graduated from Tōhoku University School of Medicine and worked as an intern in the Tōhoku University Hospital while studying for the state medical examination. On February 25, 1953, Mokichi, the father whose poems greatly inspired Kita, passed away due to cardiac asthma. In the short story "Shi" 死 (Death) published in 1964, which Kita called his only *shishōsetsu*, he wrote about Mokichi's death.

Kita passed the state medical examination in April, moved back to Tokyo, and began working in the Department of Neurology at Keiō University School of Medicine in May 1953. He worked first as an unpaid assistant and was promoted to a paid assistant in 1957. After returning to Tokyo from Sendai, Kita became more actively involved in *Bungei Shuto*. By then, some of his poems and short stories had been published in literary magazines. Around this time, he began writing *Yoru to kiri no sumi de*. Kita later recalled that this novel was especially memorable to him because it took him a very long time to complete.[34]

Although Kita was working at the university hospital, his desire to go to Germany, the country where Thomas Mann was born and grew up, never ceased. At that time in Japan, traveling to a foreign country was restricted and one had to have a specific reason to go abroad. Kita applied for the Ministry of Education study-abroad scholarship but did not pass the application screening. While he was looking for a way to go to Germany, one of his colleagues at the university hospital suggested that he become a ship's doctor. He visited one shipping company but was told that they preferred a doctor who was adept at surgery, which Kita, a psychiatrist, was not.

On November 10, 1958, Kita heard that the Japanese Fisheries Agency was seeking a doctor for one of their survey ships called the Shōyō-maru. It was scheduled to sail in a few days but the Agency had not been able to find a ship's doctor and was willing to hire any doctor regardless of his specialty. Kita quickly gave his paid assistant position to his junior colleague, took a leave of absence from Keiō University

---

34. Kita, "Sōsaku yowa," in *Kita Morio zenshū geppō*, no. 9:1, in vol. 9 of *KMZ* (1977).

Hospital. On November 15, merely five days after he first heard about the position, the ship departed with Kita on it.

Kita took with him the manuscript of *Yoru to kiri no sumi de*, but could hardly add any lines to it during his journey. He mailed installments of the account of his journey to *Bungei Shuto* from every port where the ship stopped. The installments were published under the title "Senjō nite" 船上にて (On board) from January to May 1959.

When Kita returned to Japan in April 1959, several editors who had read "Senjō nite" in *Bungei Shuto* contacted him and asked if he would be interested in writing about his voyage. However, since Kita intended to write only "pure literature," he declined their offers.[35] He returned to Keiō University Hospital as an unpaid assistant but often missed work because he suffered from a duodenal ulcer. In the summer, he went to a hot springs resort in Gunma Prefecture, hoping to make good progress on writing his novel, but it was still rough going. By the end of October, Kita decided to stop writing this difficult novel as he thought the stress would make his ulcer worse. Around that time, he was contacted by an editor of the literary magazine *Chūō Kōron* and was again asked if he would be interested in writing a travelogue. Thinking that his ulcer might get better if he were to write a "ridiculous and exorbitant"[36] essay, Kita agreed to do so. As a result of

---

35. Okuno Takeo, "'Dokutoru Manbō Kōkaiki'" in *Kita Morio no bungaku sekai* 北杜夫の文学世界 (Tokyo: Chūō Kōronsha, 1978), 118. The term "pure literature" is used here as a translation of the term *junbungaku* used by Kita in the sentence quoted above. In this discussion between Kita and Okuno Takeo, which probably took place in 1977, both used the term *junbungaku* or pure literature as opposed to *taishū bungaku* or popular literature. The opposition of pure/popular in modern Japanese literature, however, has been reexamined and questioned in recent years; and scholars have pointed out that this opposition no longer applies to many postmodern Japanese literary works such as those by Murakami Haruki and Yoshimoto Banana. It is worth noting that, as early as 1976, Shinoda Hajime wrote that Kita's works cannot be defined using the pure/popular dichotomy. See Shinoda Hajime, "Hito to bungaku" 人と文学, in *Kita Morio, Tsuji Kunio shū* 北杜夫·辻邦生集, by Kita Morio and Tsuji Kunio, *Chikuma gendai bungaku taikei* 筑摩現代文学体系 (Tokyo: Chikuma Shobō, 1976), 87:524. For a more detailed discussion on pure and popular literature, see Matthew C. Stretcher, "Purely Mass or Massively Pure? The Division Between 'Pure' and 'Mass' Literature," *Monumenta Nipponica* 51 (1996): 357–374. In this volume, the term "pure literature" is used only in the translation of a direct quotation in which the term *junbungaku* is used.

36. Okuno, "'Dokutoru Manbō Kōkaiki,'" 7.

having his essays “Senjō nite” published in *Bungei Shuto* and because he had also kept a detailed diary during his voyage, Kita found writing the travelogue to be an easy task. He finished writing it in two months and titled it *Dokutoru Manbō kōkaiki*. It was published by Chūō Kōronsha in March 1960. The book’s editor, Miyawaki Shunzō, later recalled:

> I received the following information: a young psychiatrist is traveling on the Fishery Agency’s survey ship to Europe along the African coast. It appears that he writes well. He also writes novels. It was in the spring of 1959. At that time, I was working for a publisher. It was the time that traveling abroad was a lofty dream.
>
> I was waiting for the “young psychiatrist who also writes novels” to come back to Japan, and as soon as he returned, I requested that he write a travelogue. He showed me many photos, which were all unique. I planned to turn the travelogue into a book that would contain these many photos.
>
> In about half a year, the draft was completed. It was far better than what I had expected. His writing was free-spirited and vigorous, and was filled with humor.
>
> I was fascinated by his writing, so much so that my idea of inserting photos in the travelogue somehow disappeared.
>
> The following spring, a travelogue without any pictures, which was very unusual at the time, was published. His writing captured readers’ hearts, and it immediately became a best-selling book. The book was Kita Morio’s *Dokutoru Manbō kōkaiki*.[37]

Okuno Takeo also spoke very highly of the work, describing it as the first overseas travelogue in postwar Japan that was completely free from the sense of an inferiority complex toward the West, or the elitism and nationalism that are the flip side of that inferiority complex.[38] It is true that in this work Kita employed humor to bring the grand events of the world, the nation-state, and national characteristics (including his own) down to the everyday life of laughter. He utilized various kinds of comical expressions in the work—slapstick, puns, ex-

---

37. Miyawaki Shunzō, *Tabi wa jiyū seki* 旅は自由席 (Tokyo: Shinchōsha, 1998), 243–244.
38. Okuno, “‘Dokutoru Manbō Kōkaiki,’” 114.

aggeration, and nonsensical humor—rarely seen prior to the appearance of *Dokutoru Manbō kōkaiki*. Okuno continued:

> The groundbreaking [*Dokutoru Manbō kōkaiki*] produced many ardent followers: Oda Makoto's *Nandemo mite yarō* 何でも見てやろう (I'll go everywhere and see everything), Yasuoka Shōtarō's *Amerika kanjō ryokō* アメリカ感情旅行 (A sentimental journey through America), and the work of Ōe Kenzaburō and Kaikō Takashi, whose travelogues were also very popular. Despite its simplicity and absurd humor, *Dokutoru Manbō kōkaiki* actually played a very important role in the history of Japanese literature.[39]

Beyond the varied and profound impact noted by Okuno, *Dokutoru Manbō kōkaiki* also paved the way for Inoue Hisashi and Tsutsui Yasutaka to write their comical stories using a variety of humorous expressions.

In the wake of the success of *Dokutoru Manbō kōkaiki*, Kita decided to write comical works in order to make a living while continuing to write serious literature as it might not bring him any money.[40] Kita was proud that he could utilize humor in his works. In one of his essays, he wrote:

> As a writer, I'm most proud of the fact that I employ humor, and I value humor more than other writers do. … I like all sorts of humor, whether it is of good quality or not. In literary circles, when people encounter a humorous work, they tend to criticize it by saying, "This provokes laughter of low quality" or "The writer is entertaining himself." However, when they read a serious novel, nobody says, "The writer is too serious." … My works contain all sorts of humor, including nonsensical types and slapstick, and I consider all of them very precious.[41]

He did not, however, want to become a popular writer by simply producing comical, humorous works.

> I have never wanted to become a popular writer, nor have I ever been one. There have been a few opportunities when I could have become

39. Ibid.
40. Ibid., 119.
41. Kita, "Gōman to tōkai," 475-476.

> a popular writer, such as when I published *Dokutoru Manbō kōkaiki* or *Sabishii ōsama* さびしい王様 (The lonely king). If your work becomes a best-selling book and if you keep writing something similar to it, you will become a popular writer whether you like it or not.[42]

Four years after the success of *Dokutoru Manbō kōkaiki*, Kita published his most notable work, *Nireke no hitobito*, a family saga inspired by Thomas Mann's *Buddenbrooks.* The story relates the decline over the course of three generations of a bourgeois family who owns a mental hospital in Aoyama, Tokyo. The family in *Nireke no hitobito* is modeled after the author's own family, the Saitō family.[43] Kita successfully incorporated humor into this somber work. On the back cover of the English translation of Part III, titled *The Fall of the House of Nire,* such comments as "comic masterpiece," "suffused with humor," and "a very funny novel" are highlighted. These comments seem strange because the work as a whole is a pessimistic story that depicts utterly meaningless human affairs in the flow of time we call history. Yet, humor is prominent in it. *Nireke no hitobito* is the best example of Kita's skillful incorporation of comical elements into a serious, somber work. Mishima Yukio contributed his own enthusiastic recommendation of it:

> This is one of the most important novels that has been written since the end of the war. … We could not even imagine such a towering novel that is so totally free from the unhealthy ideologies of the

42. Kita, "Sōsaku yowa," in *Kita Morio zenshū geppō,* no. 15:2, in vol. 15 of *KMZ* (1977).

43. *The House of Nire* describes the fate of the Nire family experiencing the dark times of Japan's modern era: the Great Kantō Earthquake, the second Sino-Japanese War, the Shōwa Great Depression, and the Second World War. These historical incidents are faithfully recorded, incorporating actual quotes from newspaper and magazine articles, and because of that, critics often call this novel "historical literature" or "river/saga literature." This long novel has three parts but was later translated into English by Dennis Keene in two installments: *The House of Nire* (Tokyo: Kōdansha International, 1984), which covers Parts I and II, and *The Fall of the House of Nire* (Tokyo: Kōdansha International, 1985), which is the translation of Part III. The novel was made into a TV drama and aired on TBS (Tokyo Broadcasting System) from September to October of 1965. It was later made into another TV drama and aired on NHK (*Nippon Hōsō Kyōkai*), the only public broadcaster in Japan, from April to June of 1972.

day. … This is a magnificent victory for Mr. Kita's novel. This is the novel![44]

Kita Morio and Bipolar Disorder

After the success of *Nireke no hitobito*, Kita felt sufficiently confident about making a living as a writer. At the end of 1965, he completely withdrew from working as a psychiatrist and began to devote himself to writing full-time. Yet, his life was soon to take another turn.

Saitō Yuka, Kita's daughter and an essayist, remembers peaceful days the family spent at their summer house in Karuizawa, a famous summer vacation spot in Nagano Prefecture, around 1965. "The sunlight flickered beautifully through the filter of the leaves and birds were singing in the woods. We, our family of three, had nothing to worry about. Who could have imagined that soon after, my father's life full of ups and downs would start?"[45] She is referring here to Kita's bipolar disorder, which manifested as he was approaching forty; his first manic episode was at age thirty-nine in 1966. After that time, he suffered manic and depressive bouts alternately—manic in the summer and depression in the winter at first, but he had more depressive episodes and fewer manic ones as he aged. In 1966, he wrote an essay titled "Watashi wa sōbyō de aru" 私は躁病である (I am manic), and his condition gradually became known publicly. Or rather, being a bipolar disorder patient became his trademark. People around him at first thought that because Kita wrote about his condition so comically, it was something he had made up as a marketing strategy.[46] Yoshiyuki

44. The emphasis on the last line is by Mishima Yukio. Mishima Yukio, "Nireke no hitobito" 楡家の人びと, in *Ketteiban Mishima Yukio zenshū* 決定版三島由紀夫全集 (Tokyo: Shinchōsha, 2003), 33:34.

45. Saitō Yuka, *Madogiwa OL tohoho na asa ufufu no yoru* 窓際OLトホホな朝ウフフの夜 (Tokyo: Shinchōsha, 2006), 271.

46. For example, even in 1980, more than ten years after Kita's bipolar disorder manifested, the psychiatrist Yamanaka Yasuhiro wrote that Kita's so-called bipolar disorder was not real but was a part of his humorous behavior. See Yamanaka Yasuhiro, "Kita Morio no dōwa sekai to sono himitsu," *Risō* (September 1980): 53.

Junnosuke, one of Kita's writer friends, wrote in an essay that, even though he previously wondered if Kita's depression was a mere excuse for his avoidance of working, there was no room now to doubt that Kita truly had a bipolar disorder.[47] Kita himself wrote:

> People do not seem to believe that I am truly manic-depressive. They would never understand how languid I become and how despairing I feel when I have my depressive episode. Although I have never attempted to commit suicide, my brain becomes foggy, and my body feels weary. I do not even have the energy to put toothpaste on my toothbrush so I have to ask my wife to do it for me. Not to mention, I have no energy to climb the stairs to go to my study. Writing a draft is out of the question.[48]

In another essay, he also wrote:

> It seems [that my manic phase] looks amusing to a third party. However, because I cause a lot of trouble for my family and close friends, when the episode is gone, I am filled with self-hatred, and I profoundly regret my behavior during this phase.[49]

Kita wrote in numerous essays about his strange, childish behaviors during his manic phase. For example, when he visited the United States to report on the launch of Apollo Eleven for the *Asahi Shinbun* in 1969, he decided to become a beggar and earn some strong U.S. dollars:[50]

> When I visited New York, my former junior colleague at Keiō University Hospital took care of me. He said to me, "It is very hard to make a living in a foreign country. Even if you claim to be Doctor Manbō, you cannot earn even a dollar here." So I came up with an idea to become a beggar in America and earn some money. But I wanted to do it not in a pleading way but with dignity. So I bought a

---

47. Yoshiyuki Junnosuke, "Kaitō Mabuze hakase" 怪盗マブゼ博士, in *Machikado no tabakoya made no tabi* 街角の煙草屋までの旅 (Tokyo: Kōdansha, 1979), 106.
48. Kita, "Utsu no utsu" 鬱のウツ, in *KMZ* (1977), 15:136.
49. Kita, "Sōsaku yowa," in *Kita Morio zenshū geppō,* no. 14:3, in vol. 14 of *KMZ* (1977).
50. After the Second World War, the dollar's fixed rate was set at 360 yen, and it remained at that level until 1971.

> kimono, a pen, and strips of paper, and made a pamphlet [in English] stating that I am a famous beggar and a descendant of Kaguya-hime, the Moon Princess. I tried to sell a strip of paper for a dollar. At first I attempted to beg in a park in New York City with a signboard hanging from my neck. However, at that time, the hippie culture was at its height and there were plenty of weirder people there, so I was totally ignored. Then, when I tried it at the Cape Canaveral Space Center, I thought I would be successful because many people began to gather around me but I was immediately chased out by a NASA employee.[51]

A more detailed account of the above episode was recorded in *Tsuki to jussento* 月と10セント (The moon and ten cents, 1971), one of his travelogues. In 1976, when he was in a manic phase again, he hoped to make enough money to film a movie so he invested in the stock market and almost went bankrupt. In 1977, he wrote that he was so broke that he had not been able to pay his taxes on time.[52] At around this time, Kita also attempted to set a Guinness World Record for being a healthy person who would wear pajamas for the longest period of time in the world. He refused to take off his pajamas and wore a shirt and pants on top of his pajamas every time he went out, even when he attended a wedding.[53]

In 1981, when he was again in a manic phase, he established the Republic of Manbō-Mabuze, which he claimed to be independent from Japan, identified himself as the head of the country, and called himself "Abominable Doctor Mabuze" (*Kaijin Mabuze hakase*). He created the republic's national anthem, flag, bills, coins, and even its own cigarette brand.[54] Many writers have created their own countries in their fictional works, but Kita was probably the only writer who created and actually lived in his own republic (or so he believed during

---

51. Kita, "Tsuki kojiki" 月乞食, in *Dokutoru Manbō kaisōki* どくとるマンボウ回想記 (Tokyo: Nihon Keizai Shinbun Shuppansha, 2007), 128–129.
52. Kita, "Sōsaku yowa," in *Kita Morio zenshū geppō,* no 15:3, in vol. 15 of *KMZ* (1977).
53. Kita Morio and Saitō Yuka, *Papa wa tanoshii sōutsu-byō* パパは楽しい躁うつ病 (Tokyo: Shinchōsha, 2014), 200. Saitō Yuka wrote that Kita's desire to set a Guinness World Record disappeared as his manic phase subsided.
54. Kita, "Mabuze kyōwakoku" マブゼ共和国, in *Dokutoru Manbō kaisōki* (Tokyo: Nihon Keizai Shinbun Shuppansha, 2007), 143.

his manic phase). In his comical novel titled *Totchan wa daihenjin* 父っちゃんは大変人 (My dad is an extremely eccentric man, 1981), the protagonist does all sorts of strange things, many of which reflect the ideas, plans, and behaviors that Kita came up with or carried out during his manic phase.

Although Kita wrote about his manic episodes comically and freely, it was not easy for a bipolar patient to reveal such a disorder at the time. In neuropsychiatric textbooks, bipolar disorder was listed as one of the two major endogenous psychoses, along with schizophrenic disorder, and the Japanese Medical Practitioners Law at that time stated that a medical license would be revoked should a doctor develop alcoholism or a psychiatric disorder.[55] Furthermore, people were still strongly prejudiced toward mental illnesses in Japan. Under these circumstances, Kita openly wrote about his bipolar condition, hoping to convey the message that a psychiatric patient could lead a normal life.[56] The fact that Kita Morio, a very popular, well-respected writer, had bipolar disorder and that he even depicted his condition in an entertaining manner gave great hope to other bipolar patients. Nada Inada told Kita, "Previously, when I diagnosed a patient as manic or depressive, every patient became extremely nervous. However, after you revealed your illness, a patient would look rather relieved when being diagnosed as manic-depressive and would say, 'Oh, so my condition is the same as what Mr. Kita Morio has.'"[57] Nada later reiterated this point, saying that besides making numerous contributions to the field of Japanese literature, Kita also made a great contribution to Japanese society by revealing his disorder.[58]

---

55. Nada Inada, "Kita Morio to sōutsu-byō" 北杜夫と躁鬱病, in *Tsuitō sōtokushū Kita Morio: Dokutoru Manbō bungakukan* 追悼総特集 北杜夫どくとるマンボウ文学館 (Tokyo: Kawade Shobō Shinsha, 2012), 56.
56. Kita, "Jicho o kataru: Kaitō Jibago no fukkatsu" 自著を語る：怪盗ジバゴの復活, *NEXT* 7, no. 3 (March 1990): 247.
57. Kita, "Tsuki kojiki," 129–130.
58. Nada, "Manbō, Nihonjin o kaihō, sōutsu-byō ni hikari, *Kita Morio san o itamu*" マンボウ、日本人を解放、躁鬱病に光·北杜夫さんを悼む, *Asahi Shinbun*, October 31, 2011, 30. Kita's battle with bipolar disorder was made into a TV drama titled *Dokutoru Manbō yumoa tōbyōki* どくとるマンボウユーモア闘病記 (Doctor Manbō's humorous fight against his illness), and aired on NHK in 2013.

Characteristics of Kita's Writing

Kita's bipolar disorder appeared in many of his essays, but he was also interested in a variety of things, and his wide range of interests, knowledge, and experience enabled him to successfully write in different genres and on numerous topics, whether in a comical or a serious style. As noted earlier, Kita had been collecting insects since childhood and had accumulated a vast amount of knowledge about them. He was also a big fan of *manga*, the Japanese graphic novels, and participated in script-writing for an animated film with Tezuka Osamu, who is acclaimed as the "god" of *manga*. Kita loved stories for children and he not only wrote his own nursery stories but also translated German children's stories into Japanese and classical Japanese tales into easy modern Japanese for children. He was a devoted reader of science fiction even before the genre became popular in Japan. He traveled all over the world as a ship's doctor, a travel writer, and upon invitations from the U.S. State Department and the Soviet Union of Writers. Above all else, Kita was a psychiatrist with a famous poet father and an "extraordinary" mother.[59] This knowledge and experience are reflected in many of his works in a variety of genres, from stories for small children, child–adult crossovers, and science fiction to long saga novels, overseas and domestic travelogues, and numerous humorous and comical essays in which his literary persona, Doctor Manbō or simply Manbō, holds forth on various topics. In fact, few writers surpass him in producing such a wide range of works.

Even though he wrote in such diverse genres, much of his writing appears to exhibit a common characteristic: many of Kita's works either focus on inferior or insignificant people and affairs, or are written from the perspective of an underdog. In *Nireke no hitobito*, the omniscient narrator is unable to get into the mind of Nire Kiichirō, the most significant person in the Nire family; but the same narrator is

59. Kita's mother, Saitō Teruko, became well known in Japan in her late years as an energetic elderly lady who traveled to many places in the world well into her eighties. See Kita, "Kaihi e no akogare" 海彼への憧れ, in *Haha no kage*, 154. Saitō Yuka also wrote a book about Teruko titled *Mōjo to yobareta shukujo* 猛女とよばれた淑女 (The lady who was called an extraordinary woman) in 2008.

able to depict clearly the thoughts of people who belong to the "cookhouse," the place where the ordinary, unimportant people of the Nire family gather together. The narrator's eyes are fixed on people who are labeled "inferior." In his comical Manbō series, most of the time Doctor Manbō or Manbō is depicted as a person who is unlucky and unsuccessful.[60] Very often, he fails at whatever he does or encounters troubles (often self-invited). Yet, instead of indulging in self-pity, Kita's Manbō either laughs at his problems by depicting himself comically, or he seriously tries to solve his (usually trivial) problems with all his ability and power, and the more serious he is, the funnier the situation becomes. The protagonists in many of Kita's children's stories are also underachievers; for example, ghosts who cannot scare people, a student who keeps receiving bad grades, a king who is a mere puppet of a prime minister, an uncle who does nothing but read *manga*, and an eccentric father who creates his own kingdom on his property and refuses to pay taxes but is eventually arrested by the Japanese government. Whether in a serious work or a comical one, a children's story or a long novel, Kita's central character tends to be an underdog.

Because Kita's protagonist tends to be a failure, sadness and pessimism prevail in his serious works, but this same underdog and his struggles become the source of laughter in his comical works. In some of his essays, Kita wrote that after the war he felt that nothing was of any significance, and such pessimism can be observed in his somber works. However, Kita was also able to portray his belief that, when nothing or no individual is significant, there exists no insignificance either; and that is why his characters, especially in his comical works, are free from self-pity. Yet, even in these, Kita casts a benevolent eye toward lonely, ordinary, insignificant people. Those who feel vulnerable, lonely, and insignificant are, from time to time, comforted and encouraged through Kita's work, sometimes by laughing at a charac-

---

60. Reed M. Peterson writes, "In his Manbō series, … Manbō holds himself up as an exaggerated version of the human imperfection and struggles of life that each person born into mortality experiences." Reed M. Peterson, "*An Account of My Perplexities: The Humorous Essays of Kita Morio*" (PhD diss., University of Arizona, 2009), 254.

ter who seems just like them, and sometimes by feeling the writer's compassionate eyes trained on a character who seems as insignificant as they feel they are. It is not surprising that his works were very popular during his time: they have enduring value because they speak to so many parts of the human spirit.

Asked once for his opinion about receiving a medal of honor, Kita replied that he was not adequate material for receiving a medal and that a cap from an ordinary soda bottle would be good enough for him.[61] The Japanese government, however, did not agree with Kita's self-assessment. In 2009 Saitō Yuka revealed that a few years earlier Kita had been offered an award bestowed by the Japanese emperor, but he had declined it.[62] In 2011, one month after his passing, Kita was posthumously awarded The Order of the Rising Sun, Gold Rays with Neck Ribbon (*kyokujitsu chūjushō* 旭日中綬章), an award given by the Japanese government to people who achieve outstanding accomplishments in their field and are thereby granted the Junior Fourth Rank (*jushii* 従四位).[63] Although Kita's body of works itself proves that Kita was a distinguished writer, it is gratifying that his great contribution to the field of Japanese literature and to society has been publicly recognized in this way.

---

61. "'Kunshō hoshii' to kigyō, gyōkai ga honsō" 「勲章ほしい」と企業·業界が奔走, *Asahi Shinbun* (evening edition), November 8, 1986, 7. Years ago, Japanese children would affix a soda bottle cap to a shirt, pretending it was an important medal.

62. Kita and Saitō, *Papa wa tanoshii sōutsu-byō*, 194. It is not clear when and what award Kita was offered. It has been speculated that the award was *Shiju hōshō* (紫綬褒章: Medal of Honor with Purple Ribbon), which is given to those whose contribution to society in science, the arts, or sports is considered outstanding. A recipient of the medal is selected by the Japanese government but the medal is bestowed by the emperor.

63. The Order of the Rising Sun, established in 1875, is Japan's oldest award bestowed by the government. It was initially created to award those who contributed to national or public services. Now it is awarded to those who have had outstanding achievements in their field, such as those who have contributed to the stability and development of international communities, promoted schools or social education, or promoted culture or sports. For more information on the eligibility criteria set by Japanese government for decorations and medals, see Cabinet Office, Government of Japan, "Kunshō no juyo kijun" 勲章の授与基準, last modified December 26, 2006. http://www8.cao.go.jp/shokun/seidokaikaku/juyokijun.pdf

About This Book

My first experience with the world of Kita Morio was in middle school when I read *Dokutoru Manbō kōkaiki*. I found it extremely humorous; the comical expressions in his work were fascinating to me, and soon I began reading more and more of the Manbō series. Then one day while browsing the shelves of a local bookstore, I found another book by Kita called *Yūrei*. I purchased the book, expecting it to be another comical story in the same vein as the other works of his that I had read. I still remember my disappointment and surprise when I started to read *Yūrei* and found nothing funny at all in the beginning of the book. In frustration, I skimmed through the entire book trying to find something comical but to no avail. Despite that, I soon found that I had become captivated by the beautiful depiction of nature and the protagonist's childhood memories, which allowed me to immerse myself in the world that Kita had created in *Yūrei*. At the same time, Kita Morio began to come across to me as a writer of more depth. It was the versatility of his writing style, which had become apparent to me after reading *Yūrei*, that made me want to read more of his works.

The purpose of this volume is to introduce, to people in the English language arena, Kita Morio as a prolific writer who was not confined to a single genre, but instead, freely expressed himself across a wide range of literary genres. The thirteen stories translated here represent that variety. "Death" 死 is autobiographical fiction; "At the Mouth of the River" 河口にて, "The Captain" 船長, "Tadpole" おたまじゃくし, and "Yellow Ship" 黄いろい船 are serious, somber works of fiction; "I Am Manic" 私は躁病である, "My Mother's Home Cooking" 母の味, and "On Layabouts" なまけもの論 are comical essays; "Improper" 不倫, "In the Hollow" うつろの中, and "Shopping" 買物 are science fiction; and finally "Himalayan Hyōtantsugi" ヒマラヤのヒョウタンツギ and "The Red Ghost and the White Ghost" 赤いオバケと白いオバケ are stories for children. It is not an easy task to properly introduce Kita Morio through such a small selection of his extremely large body of work, but I have chosen these stories because they are representative of the various genres found in his shorter works.

I decided upon the title "Red Ghost, White Ghost" for this book. The title is taken from "The Red Ghost and the White Ghost" included in this book, and it is also an homage to one of his unfinished works titled *Shiroi obake to akai obake* 白いオバケと赤いオバケ (*The White Ghost and the Red Ghost*) which was intended as a serious, philosophical nursery story for adults. Kita had long been interested in ghosts. When he was experiencing manic episodes around 1990, he often painted "red and white ghosts."[64] In 1995, he claimed that he had written the beginning part of the story *Shiroi obake to akai obake*, and that it already numbered two hundred and thirty pages.[65] In a book published in 2001, he talked about the story yet again, saying that he would have really liked to finish it: the story would have been at least two-thousand pages once it was done, but he did not have the physical strength to complete it.[66] I sincerely hope Kita Morio would have approved of my choice for the title of this book.

It is my hope that my translations will serve to introduce readers to the full range of this unique, remarkably versatile writer's work.

---

64. See Kita and Saitō, "Papa wa tanoshii sōutsu-byō," 202. One of his paintings is on the cover of this voume.
65. Kita, "Jicho o kataru," 247.
66. Kita, *Manbō yuigonjō*, 57. The beginning of the story was published in the literary magazine *Chūō Kōron bungei tokushū* in 1995 as a serialized novel. Unfortunately the story was not completed after two installments. "Shiroi obake to akai obake" no. 1 and no. 2 are in *Chūō Kōron bungei tokushū* 12, no. 1 (Spring 1995) and no. 2 (Summer 1995), respectively.

stories & essays

i am manic

Watashi wa sōbyō de aru

私は躁病である

I was very energetic and extroverted long ago when I wrote *Doctor Manbō at Sea*. I was frowned upon for my unrestrained, even reckless remarks.

Then I grew older and became antisocial. It was such a bother for me to talk to anyone. When I had to converse, the only words out of my mouth were "yeah, yeah" or "uh-huh." When I was interviewed, I didn't talk or even listen. When the interviewer stopped talking, I would say "I see" and drink more sake.

I assumed this happened simply because I had grown older. I thought perhaps it was time I gave up my literary persona as Manbō and proposed to a publisher that my next book be titled "An Account of Dying Manbō."

That was several years ago, and suddenly this April my energy returned. Everyone is cyclothymic to a greater or lesser extent. In other words, we all experience periods of feeling high and low. Extreme cases are diagnosed as bipolar disorder. In my case, I'm essentially schizothymic, but I suspect I'm also affected by a big cyclothymic wave every several years.

The first thing I thought about after regaining my energy was to build up my physical strength in order to prepare for writing a long novel that I wanted to begin in one month. I am thirty-nine years old, but because I hadn't been exercising, my physical strength, according to my own diagnosis as a medical doctor, was that of a man in his late forties.

I attempted just a simple exercise, but it hurt so much when I tried to raise my leg, I couldn't stamp my foot on the ground. After several days, however, my flexibility gradually improved. Next, I began running, first charging around in rubber flip-flops, before I purchased a pair of proper running shoes. I thought of buying workout clothes as well, but I refrained for fear that I would want to participate in the Olympics.

As I got into better shape, I regretted those years of dull idleness and felt like spitting on my old unhealthy lifestyle.

The problem was that my energy kept expanding—into a manic disorder. I abruptly went to Kyoto to gather research, bought far too many books, decided to add on a room to store the books, bought thirty rolls of toilet paper ... I even purchased some stock on a whim that flashed into my head and consequently lost all my money. Ordinarily I might be considered an incapacitated person or a candidate for a mental hospital. Because I am a psychiatrist, however, I am able to lead a somewhat normal life.

In Karuizawa, I went horseback riding for the first time in a long while. It felt good, but later I suffered from body aches that made me realize my regular exercise routine wasn't enough. Immediately I visited my old riding club again. I took out my riding boots, which had accumulated dust in my closet. Because I hadn't worn them for seven or eight years, the leather was very stiff, plus my feet had lost their youthful shape, so the boots didn't fit at all. That very same day I ordered custom-made boots, requesting that they be a little roomy.

Even with my disorder, there was a little intellect remaining in me, and I remembered that Mr. Mishima Yukio had once written, "I realized that horseback riding would surely be detrimental to my production." I called and asked him about this, and he told me, "That's what I thought then, but now I think otherwise." I used to laugh at him behind his back when he engaged in all his sports, but now I admit he was absolutely right. He is an extraordinarily gifted man who won't be dying anytime soon because he has been exercising. I am filled with horror when I imagine him living on and becoming a super eccentric centenarian. It's good to occasionally seek advice from such a great man but keep a respectful distance. By the way, I don't think he could win a Nobel Prize easily. It is an honorary award and is pretty much only given to those with one foot in the grave. However, thanks to his physical training, Mr. Mishima looks very young, even like a boy to foreigners' eyes. If the Japanese literati want to see him win a Nobel, they should ask him to stop exercising, grow a white beard, and stoop over and totter along with a cane.

I don't play golf. I know walking outside is good for the body, but golf is for old folks. Younger ones should play tougher, faster sports. I would rather hit my wife with a pestle if I want to swing a stick, and it would be cheaper to play pinball if I want to put a ball into a hole. Besides, it's not acceptable for a grown man to make a woman carry his clubs.[1] I realize that making a good shot on a golf course is more difficult and more satisfying than hitting a home run in a baseball game, but it doesn't matter. I just cannot hit the ball; I wouldn't play such a silly sport.

Anyway, my manic disorder shows no sign of subsiding. At one social gathering, I met Ms. Satō Aiko[2] and said to her, "I thought you might already be an old lady, but look how glamorous you are." I told another female writer, "I would love to see your strip show." I swear I never intended to say these things, but the words just jumped out of my mouth.

What's most troublesome is that I tell every woman I meet, "I'd like to make you my mistress." At this rate, by the time my manic episode does subside, I'll have dozens of mistresses and will have to become a sultan.

---

1. In Japan, country club caddies tend to be women.
2. Satō Aiko 佐藤愛子 (1923–) is a novelist and was Kita's friend for more than fifty years.

By the way, regarding the long novel that I mentioned earlier—I chose May 1st to commence my work, which was May Day, my birthday, and which happened to fall on a Sunday. In my mania, I hoisted the Z flag[3] to inspire myself—that is, I posted on my wall "No brooding! Work! Define, eliminate, fashion, complete!" This comes from Thomas Mann's "A Weary Hour."[4] I used the Z flag only once before, when I began writing *The House of Nire*.

My plan for the day was to spend an hour running and exercising, and five to six hours writing. The rest of the day was for research and rest. I was secretly satisfied as my lifestyle came to look like that of a healthy foreign writer. On the day I was to commence writing, I woke up before noon, drank a glass of juice and took herbal medicine, exercised for an hour, ate ramen noodles for lunch, took some vitamin pills, and finally sat down at my desk. When I wrote down the title in large characters, I used too much force and tore the paper.

But then I began the book. In my manic state, my pen never stopped moving. I had planned to write five pages a day, but I wrote seven and a half pages in just one afternoon. It seemed disastrous to keep writing like this, as there would be no way I could produce decent text. I would end up with a piece of junk.

Probably the only thing I could do, I thought, was to finish the manuscript this quickly and then take antimanic medication. Then, once my mania calmed down, I could carefully edit my draft.

At dinnertime, after drinking a bottle of sake, I realized how exhausted my body was. I had abused both my body and my brain during the day, so I couldn't work at night the way I could before. I took a bath at nine-thirty and went to bed early.

This state of overdrive is likely to continue for a while. For your own sake, my best advice is to steer clear of me.

---

3. At the Battle of Tsushima in 1905 during the Russo-Japanese War, Admiral Tōgō Heihachirō 東郷平八郎 hoisted the signal flag for the letter Z (Z 旗) on his flagship, Mikasa 三笠, in order to raise the morale of the soldiers.

4 "A Weary Hour" (*Schwere Stunde*), by Thomas Mann (1875–1955), is a short story published in 1905.

shopping

Kaimono

買物

I played a game, assuming the man was not mentally ill.

I am a doctor at a public mental hospital. There are about four hundred and fifty patients but only six doctors, including the director and part-timers who commute from a university hospital two days a week. That leaves the full-time physicians like me responsible for nearly one hundred patients each.

Our situation is pathetic. In addition to seeing inpatients, we examine outpatients and are also expected to conduct our own research so we make only cursory examinations on our rapid rounds. If I spent any reasonable time with each patient, I could see no more than five a day; it would take me a month to get to all of the patients in my care. In other words, inpatients would receive thorough examination from their doctors only once a month.

That could explain why Mikita, who is quite possibly sane, or so I believed, had been confined in this hospital. He was classified as a paranoid schizophrenic, but that's often difficult to diagnose because a patient who has a certain delusion may not lack intelligence in other areas and otherwise be quite normal. For instance, a woman who claims to have been raped by her gynecologist may not be delusional.

But if she claims to have been raped many times, her story may defy credibility. Patients who insist on saying something absurd such as "I am the crown prince's lover" or "I married Elizabeth Taylor" are usually admitted to the hospital.

Mikita claimed that he was assembling a time machine. If that was all there was to it, it would be hard to judge whether or not he was psychotic. However, the assistant professor who brought Mikita to the hospital didn't think a time machine was possible to create, and so Mikita was diagnosed as mentally ill and admitted. Mikita, a thirty-year-old assistant in the university's physics laboratory, had begun to create a strange machine using the school's materials without permission.

The hospital did not consider his condition unusual. Patients' delusions often reflect the time period in which they live. It is also common for a patient to suffer a paranoid delusion that someone is watching him. In the past, many patients claimed that they were being monitored by someone hiding in their attic. In modern times, many insisted that someone was watching them through the TV screen. Some said they were exposed to radiation and others claimed they were extraterrestrials. Now that science fiction is so popular, psychiatric patients are among the first to incorporate it into their lives. Thus, the arrival of our time machine maker wasn't all that remarkable, just generating a few jokes among the doctors in the conference room.

I was interested in Mikita because I am not good at conducting conventional research but I have a habit of trying to make all-or-nothing breakthroughs. Once, I invented a hiccup therapy. Since stimulation therapies such as insulin or electric shock are often used to treat mental patients, I tried giving my patient a drug that strongly stimulated his diaphragm, inducing powerful artificial hiccups. According to my theory, the patient should have been cured, but unfortunately his continuous hiccups never stopped so I couldn't interview him to evaluate the results of the therapy, and I was severely reprimanded by my boss. In order to restore my good name, I next made a huge coil. I had a patient climb into it and applied electrical current. In this case,

I am certain that the patient's condition did improve. It's just that, when we took him out of the coil, he fell off its ladder and broke his jaw, and he is still unable to speak. My boss was enraged and ordered me never to conduct any new experiments again. But I know that the patient got better. The beauty of the treatment was that the coil was wound to the right.[1]

Well, it was only natural for me as an aspiring inventor to be interested in a patient who claimed to have built a time machine. I never believed that such a machine was possible, but it was fun to fantasize about. I would like to travel a hundred years into the future and bring back more advanced therapeutic instruments or medications for mental illness, and I enjoyed imagining the surprise on the face of the boss I hated.

Mikita happened to be under the direct care of my boss, so I went to see him while the senior doctor was out. Mikita was a skinny young man around my age, with a vacant expression on his face. He was on large doses of chlorpromazine to reduce delusions.

"No matter how much medication you give me, it won't help," he said as soon as he saw me in my white coat. "I'm not sick." He added, "The medication makes me sleepy and I can't stand it. If I keep taking it, I will certainly become a real mental patient."

I learned nothing from his self-evaluation. A crazy person would make these comments, but so would a normal person.

When I looked at him, though, I felt something. What on earth is the difference between insanity and sanity? Isn't what most people think at a given time considered normal? In the medieval era, those who believed in witches were considered normal. If one tried to draw a line between extreme insanity and, so to speak, extreme normality (I know this is a weird phrase), where would that line be? As doctors, we encounter many insane people. If we see a patient with a typical paranoia, we are very often guided by our intuition even when our so-

---

1. "Wound to the left" (*hidarimaki* 左巻き) is Japanese slang for an insane person; presumably the narrator believed that a charge from a coil wound to the right would counteract insanity.

called science cannot pinpoint the problem. If a person is mad, we sense it immediately.

When I saw Mikita's face and heard his voice, I didn't sense anything crazy about him.

I took him to my private office and offered him a cup of tea. I didn't mention anything about his illness. I told him that I too liked to invent things and I'd like to have him teach me physics. While we chatted, Mikita let down his guard, spoke lucidly and eloquently, and even began to smile. He said that this was the first time he'd been treated like a human being since he'd been admitted to the hospital. I subtly asked him questions about magnetism, entropy, and so on. His answers were precise and proved that his intelligence was not impaired. Still, as to whether he was delusional, that remained unresolved.

"By the way," I asked, "I heard you're able to make a time machine. Is that right?"

"Yes, probably," he replied, grinning.

"So, tell me about it. How is time structured?"

"Time?" he said, "There is not a single scholar on earth who can precisely explain time. Frankly, I don't understand it at all."

"Can you make a time machine without understanding time?"

"It's the same for you doctors," he remarked with a grin. "You treat mental illness without understanding it. With electroshock, you only know that it works, but I've heard that you don't know why it works."

"There is a theoretical explanation, but it's just a hypothesis."

"If hypotheses counted, there are plenty of them about time. For instance, according to one hypothesis, time is a spiral. Normally the spiral takes decades to make a circle, but if we compress it and connect one part of the coil to another with a wire, we could use that to travel from the present decades ahead or behind us. Maybe decades could become hundreds or thousands of years."

I changed the topic and asked him about the principle behind his time machine. He insisted he knew nothing about it, but he said that one evening he had a very vivid dream in which he saw a blueprint for the machine. I was disappointed by that. The more I talked to him, however, the more I was convinced that he was not crazy. He may simply have been obsessed by an innocent mania, in which case there was no need to lock him up in a mental hospital.

I said, "I don't think you are sick, but using materials at the university without permission was wrong, don't you agree?"

"That was a mistake," he admitted. "I was impatient. Since I had no clue how a time machine might work, I just had to actually build one. If I didn't try, I'd never prove anything. I felt pressured."

"All right. If you promise me you won't make the same mistake again, I'll tell you how to get out of here."

Mikita was not my patient, but I wanted to get back at my boss, so I explained in detail the tricks for getting discharged. First, Mikita would have to admit that he was sick and ask his doctors why his mind was so strange. I also told him how he should behave, and how he should explain himself, and so on.

"Oh, I came up with those ideas a long time ago," Mikita said.

"Then why didn't you act on them?"

"I just felt I shouldn't. I felt bad if I deceived you doctors," he replied.

I chuckled ruefully. "Well, I wish you a successful return to the outside world. Next time, choose a safer place to assemble your time machine. And if you do create one, let me know—I'd like to take part in the experiment."

"Of course, doctor."

After that, I was busy for about a month. The next time I visited the ward where Mikita was, I found that he had been discharged. I checked his medical record and read my hated boss's handwriting: "Delusion has totally disappeared. A reportable case of the positive effect of chlorpromazine. Discharged."

I couldn't help but grin.

A few days later, as I came back to my apartment in the evening, I saw a man waiting at my front door. It was Mikita.

"What happened?" I asked.

"Doctor, thanks to your advice, I got out of the hospital," he replied. "And I've decided to follow your suggestion."

"Suggestion? What was that?"

"To choose a safe place to build my time machine. You were right, doctor. If I assemble the machine just anywhere, I'd have to go back to the hospital. So I've chosen a safe place."

"A safe place? Where?"

"I'll live with you and assemble the time machine here. I'll be safe here, right, doctor? You'll contribute some money, won't you?"

I was taken by surprise, but for some reason I let him into my apartment.

"How much do you think it will cost to build?"

"If I follow my first blueprint, billions."

"That's impossible!" I waved my hands to stop him.

"But it's really strange," he continued without paying attention to me. "The first blueprint I saw in my dream was elaborate and precise. Then, when I was forced to take the medication at the hospital, I began dreaming of simpler and simpler drawings. Figuratively speaking—first I dreamed about a jet plane, and now it's just a glider or a model airplane."

"So, how much would the model airplane cost?"

"Let me see … probably twenty or thirty thousand yen, depending on how I do it."

"That's too cheap," I said. "I wouldn't trust a time machine that was built for only twenty thousand yen."

"Of course, its performance wouldn't be very good," he conceded. "It wouldn't be able to travel freely but might go to only one point in time. Even so, that'd be wonderful, wouldn't it?"

After a lot of conversation, I let him live with me. It is hard to live in this world without having dreams, and building a time machine for twenty thousand yen is a bargain compared to the cost of going out drinking in bars.

I was fairly satisfied with merely having the dream, but Mikita started to build something in my apartment. He bought several aluminum basins, explaining that they would form the outside wall of the machine. He also purchased vacuum tubes, batteries, and copper wire.

"What's the power source for the machine?" I asked in fun. "Do you create a strong magnetic field, or do you need lots of electricity?"

He responded that though he would need to use some dry-cell batteries, the main power source would be a rubber band.

"A rubber band?"

"Yep," he said. "This machine is very simple, you know. Think about a model airplane. It flies with a rubber band."

"Oh, I see," I said, as if I were stupid. After all, it would cost only twenty thousand yen.

While I worked at the hospital, Mikita labored diligently and completed the machine in less than a month.

"This is a crude model, so it can't go more than ten to twenty years forward or back," he said. "I hope it'll go to the future. I wonder how much the world will have advanced by then. I bet twenty years from now, mental hospitals will have machines that can identify someone like me as normal."

I doubted that.

Anyhow, we decided to experiment with the machine. We brought it discreetly to the grounds of a nearby shrine. Fortunately, our first machine was a fold-up one, so it was fairly convenient to transport. Behind the shrine was a little cliff where few people came to. As long as the shrine and the cliff were here, we felt, the machine would not arrive in the past or future on, for example, a busy street. This seemed okay for a preliminary run of only a decade or two.

Mikita said, "Twist this rubber band to start the machine. Twisting more won't make the machine go farther. Once it reaches a different time, it will bounce back to the starting point because of the distortion of time caused by time travel. But we should be able to stay there for about twenty-four hours. We can't travel more widely in time when our engine is just a rubber band."

He assembled the machine in a grove on top of the cliff, stocked it with some canned food and bread in case of emergency, and climbed in. Not much room was left, but that was all right, as I was not planning to join him.

"Here I go," he said, extending his hand to me. I shook it with a serious look on my face. The best thing was to enjoy the drama, I thought, especially since it was so inexpensive.

The lid of the machine closed. I stepped back, though I didn't really believe it would move. To my surprise, the machine started to zoom. I could not believe what I saw next: the machine with Mikita in it began spinning around like a top. It picked up momentum, eventually spinning into a gray mist, and then, nothing.

I stood frozen. I stretched my hand into the space where the machine had been. I felt nothing. Mikita and the machine had disappeared.

I wandered around in shock for a long time. I remembered Mikita saying that he would stay for about twenty-four hours, so there was nothing for me to do but go home and drink whisky. That night I had strange dreams about Mikita. In one dream, the machine defied our expectations and went into the future thousands of years from now, where Mikita was put in a zoo. In another, he went tens of thousands of years into the past and got trampled by a dinosaur.

The next day, I took a day off from work and went to the cliff behind the shrine early in the morning. About twenty-four hours after the machine had vanished, a swirling gray mist began to form. It spun more slowly until it eventually stopped. The lid opened and Mikita stuck his head out.

He looked tired. He had white powder scattered on his clothes.

"How was it? Have you really been somewhere, I mean, to the past or the future?" I shouted.

"It was a success," was all he said. He did not seem very happy.

"I traveled about twenty years, not to the future but to the past. It was right after the war, and there was nothing there. Damn it, I wish I could have gone to the future."

"Don't say that. This is an amazing achievement. Let's go back to the apartment so you can tell me the story."

According to Mikita, the time machine landed in the dead grass on top of the cliff behind the same shrine. The shrine itself had not changed much, but when he looked down from there, he saw the town was in ruins, half burned and with shanties everywhere. The people he saw walking around were dirty and cold.

He walked to a nearby train station, took out his wallet to buy a newspaper, and discovered that his money had all turned into confetti.

He told me, "This also happened to my tissues. It seems that something abnormal happens to paper when going against the current of time."

When he took out a coin to buy a newspaper, the woman selling papers gave him a suspicious look. "What kind of coin is this?" she said. "A hundred yen? I've never seen such a thing."

He hurriedly left, but not before seeing the date on the newspaper: March 26, 1946.

The front of the station was crowded with black-market stalls selling steamed potatoes, dried potatoes, peanuts, rice balls, work gloves, socks, pots and pans, and canteens. He went back to the time machine to get some of his canned food, and as soon as he put the cans on the street they got sold. Thus he acquired some ten-yen bills with a picture of the Diet Building. Most bank bills had been converted to these new ones, but some "bull bills," with certificates attached to them, were still in circulation.[2] With these, he could take a train and have a look around. At one station, he was doused with DDT, which was being used to prevent typhus.

"Look. I brought back some currency as evidence. Here it is."

"Oh, these old bills ..." I said. "But didn't you say paper turned into confetti when traveling in time?"

"That happened going into the past, but not on the way back to the

2. The conversion to the new currency took place in 1946; however, to cope with the shortage of new bank bills, existing bills with certificate stickers were considered valid. A "bull bill" was an old 10-yen bill with a picture of a bull on it.

present. See, this paper is intact, too." He had the newspaper wrapping from dried potatoes, and I could easily read the date of 1946.

After this, I became serious about the machine. We performed many experiments. I stopped going to work and began time traveling instead. We discovered some unfortunate things:

We could only go into the past but never the future.

We could only go from about February of 1946 to February of the following year. Within this range, we could not control the day we would arrive. That was all up to God.

Paper always became tattered going to the past, but it was fine coming back to the present. Nothing but paper was affected in this way.

The time machine would always return to the present in twenty-four hours; if we were not on board, we might get left in the past. We also found that we couldn't go from the past into a more distant past.

You might ask why we didn't raise money to develop an improved machine, but Mikita had stopped dreaming of blueprints. It was sheer chance that he was able to create even this very basic time machine, so we decided to make the most of it even with its limitations. We were both so materialistic that all we thought about next was how we might make a profit with it.

The problem was that 1946 had nothing to offer us. If we took a lot of canned goods and sold them at high prices, inflation would make our earnings worth little in the present. And what inventions could we bring home from 1946—a cigarette roller? a toaster?

Mikita grumbled, "I wish we could go to the future so we could bring back a piece of equipment to cure cancer. Or if we could go farther into the past, we could find things that would be valuable antiques now."

"Wait, how about gambling?" I exclaimed. "They must've had horse racing back then. If we could obtain a newspaper from the past and checked the results …"

"That won't work. We wouldn't know exactly what date we'd arrive. If we could find all the 1946 and 1947 newspapers and bring them back to the past with us, we'd check the newspaper of the day, sell our canned food, then use the proceeds at the racetrack. But the newspapers would get shredded on the trip, and we wouldn't be able to read the racing results."

"How about buying stock?"

"That's no good, either. It might appreciate, but the initial stock we could purchase would be worth so little to start with. A company would allow us to purchase more stock during the next twenty years, but we wouldn't have the opportunity to purchase it."

Meanwhile, we continued the small business we had conducted on past trips. We'd load up as many cheap canned goods and socks as we could and go into the past. When we tried selling in black markets, the hoodlums who ran the places would threaten us, so we'd sell on the street. Because the labels always got ruined, we had to open one can as a sample. This was at a time when there was almost nothing available, so we easily sold everything we brought. With the proceeds, we purchased postage stamps and brought them home. The value of stamps from that time had grown in value, which earned us some money but not a lot. It would have been different with fine jewelry or antiques, but we couldn't afford such items with our meager earnings from canned food.

I suggested that we take a transistor radio or a small television to the past, but Mikita disagreed. "That would alter the past, which would affect the present. It would be dangerous."

"But weren't you hoping to bring inventions from the future back to the present? Isn't it the same thing?"

"True, but now we know we can't go to the future. Anyway, I don't feel good about it. My subconscious tells me so, and the time machine was the product of my subconscious in the first place, you know."

"But we've already intervened in the past. We took canned food and brought back postage stamps."

"Those small things can't have much effect. Bringing televisions to 1946 would be different and dangerous, as they were only invented much later."

I struck my knee when the idea came to me.

"Hey, we didn't think about something very important. In 1946, we were still kids. Why don't we find ourselves, or my father who died three years ago, and give them some advice? For instance, we could advise them to buy stock because the Korean War would start soon …"

"That's even worse," Mikita said, shaking his head. "Nobody would believe us. Anyway, meeting ourselves in the past is a terrible idea, the most dangerous thing we could do. I'm absolutely opposed."

"Here's another idea: why don't I memorize as many historical events as I can and then go stay in the past and be a great prophet? But wait, would there be two of me existing at the same time? One is thirty-three years old and the other is fifteen—which one would be the real me?"

I grasped my head in confusion. Mikita looked at me sternly and just shook his head.

One day I was browsing through a magazine and found the autobiography of Tanzawa Jirō. Nowadays, everyone knows of this artistic genius. He recently had a major one-man show, and the prices of his paintings were going through the ceiling.

Yet he was very poor at the start of his career. After the war he was on the verge of starvation and could not even afford paint. Only after his painting was accepted at the Nitten Exhibition for the first time, in 1947, could he survive as an artist.

Mikita was complaining, "Of all the possible points in time, why do we always go to the same boring time just after the war? I'm even more convinced that time really is a helix. Let me explain to you—there's the argument that if a time machine were to be created in the future, a time traveler from the future could appear at any time in history. But we haven't encountered any time travelers, and therefore people concluded that making a time machine was impossible." Then he added: "Records indicate, however, that time travelers appeared at one point in the past. So it makes perfect sense that even an advanced time machine could travel only within a limited time period, because it would only go from one point of the spiral to another."

I was more focused on the magazine article than on listening to Mikita. "Hey, Mikita, you understand paintings, don't you?"

"Paintings? Not really."

"But you must know Tanzawa Jirō, right?"

"I've heard the name. What about him?"

"Look at this. It was in 1947 when Tanzawa Jirō's work was first accepted at the Nitten Exhibition. That's right after our time machine usually arrives. After that, he began to make his name as a painter and eventually became one of Japan's premier artists. But, before that, he was terribly poor and thought of giving up painting. This is a great opportunity for us."

"Opportunity? How so?"

"You idiot. We could go find the unknown, impoverished Tanzawa Jirō, purchase his paintings for next to nothing, and bring them back here where they are extremely valuable."

"I see." Mikita had a serious look on his face and crossed his arms.

We carefully planned our next move. The plan seemed foolproof. We traveled to the past frequently, sold canned food, and hid our proceeds on the grounds of the shrine, all the while diligently trying to locate where Tanzawa Jirō was living in 1946. This turned out more difficult than we had supposed, because he was very obscure at that time. Finally, Mikita pretended to be a newspaper reporter and called the famous Tanzawa Jirō of the present time.

"I am working on your biographical sketch," he lied. "Where were you living after the war?"

"I drifted from town to town after I was discharged from military service. I didn't have my own place," the master replied.

"Do you remember where you were living in 1946?"

"1946 … I think it was in front of the Nishi-Ogikubo Station. There was a public bathhouse nearby, and I was renting a room from the Nishida family."

"Do you remember the address?"

"I don't recall. Do you need the address for my biography?"

"No, no. Thank you for your time."

Mikita hurriedly hung up, but his purpose had been accomplished.

Back in the past, he soon located the house. It was a dirty, half-ruined two-story house that had not been bombed in the war, and he confirmed that a young man named Tanzawa Jirō was boarding on the second floor. When Mikita stopped by, the young man was out and he couldn't wait, as it was close to the time for the time machine to return to the present.

On my next trip, I found Tanzawa Jirō at home. Young Tanzawa was very pale, but his sunken eyes were keenly alert.

I glanced around the house. There was an unfinished painting in the middle of the room. It was an abstract that looked like a chaotic dark lump. Five or six small paintings were set against one wall, and a canteen, a toaster, and some sweet potatoes and orange peels were scattered on the tatami mats covering the floor. This poverty was just what I had expected to see.

"What do you want with me?" the pale young man asked, a glint in his sharp eyes.

"I'm interested in buying some of your paintings." I put on a very high-handed air.

"My paintings?" He seemed surprised. "My paintings are not for sale," he murmured. His voice sounded faint and trailed off, almost lost in his hunger and despair.

"I didn't come here to argue with you." From my pocket I took out a thick bundle of ten-yen bills that we had stashed at the shrine. I tossed the wad of money onto the tatami. "I'll take all of your paintings. Yes or no?"

He hesitated, but then weakly nodded. I saw ecstasy and sadness in his eyes at the same time.

I was gathering up his paintings when he abruptly asked, "Are you going to take this one, too?"

"Of course."

"But it's unfinished."

"That's fine."

I said no more. All the paintings were small, and I had no problem carrying them. I left the young man, still rather dazed, in the house.

Mikita was, of course, very happy when I returned to the present.

"One, two, three ... six of them. These will bring us a fortune."

"If I could go back just a few days later, I could get a few more."

"Don't be greedy—these are enough. They all have his signature. And this one is unfinished, so maybe it will command a higher price."

The next day, we visited an art dealer. We were excited and had high expectations.

We could not believe what we heard. The dealer said, "Tanzawa Jirō? Never heard of him. Is this his work? We only deal with artists of major stature, as you can see."

We were shocked and immediately went to another dealer, but the result was the same. We soon realized there was no painter named Tanzawa Jirō, or at least not one who was famous.

"What the hell is happening?" I mumbled.

"I don't know," Mikita replied, disheartened.

After a silence, he looked rather grave and said, "We might have interfered in the past too much. That's why the present has changed."

"What do you mean?"

"It's that unfinished painting. I thought I'd seen it before, and now I think it was the one accepted at the Nitten Exhibition. Because we took it away, he didn't get into Nitten and so he never became famous."

"Come on, we only took six paintings. We did him a favor. He couldn't sell anything, he was weak with malnutrition, and we left him a lot of money. He could have bought food or more paints, so he could have produced more paintings than ever."

"But it didn't go that way," Mikita said, looking disappointed. "The fact is that Tanzawa Jirō has disappeared. The unfinished painting might have been the key determinant of his future destiny. Or he might have bought liquor with the windfall we provided; maybe he gave himself up to drinking."

"What did happen to him?"

"I don't know. He might have starved to death or just quit painting," Mikita said pensively. "What I do know is that we've buried a genius."

"What should we do?"

"Hmm. If we go back to the past again, we might arrive at a time after you purchased the paintings and we could give them back. But I'm not even so sure we can travel through time any more. I have a feeling the time machine is about to break down. My subconscious has been telling me so."

"Can you make a new machine?"

"Probably not. I haven't had any more dreams lately …"

Then Mikita looked back at me, and said with a thin smile, "After all this, we'd better go back to the mental hospital, don't you think? I mean, both of us. Now you'll be a patient too."

tadpoles

Otamajakushi

おたまじゃくし

■■■

It was before the Second Sino-Japanese War began, a time when everyone thought the world was at peace.

"Distance, threeee hundre-e-ed," a child sang out.

"Fire!" an adult said.

And they began shooting: on a narrow path in a field of golden mustard flowers, they lay on their stomachs holding bamboo sticks and opened fire against the enemy troops hiding in the faraway oak woods.

"Bang, bang!" shouted the boy.

"Bang," the man uttered quietly.

For the boy, the bamboo stick was a rifle, and he aimed it carefully with one eye closed. He could hear enemy bullets cutting through the air and see landmines kicking up a cloud of dust around him. He ducked his head to the ground, and then, having miraculously survived the enemy's attacks, he began firing his bamboo rifle again. While shooting, his rifle suddenly became a machine gun and the boy was mowing down enemy soldiers right and left.

He jumped up and took a few steps forward, but the next moment he flopped forward on the ground to fire his machine gun again.

"Ba, ba, ba, Ba-ba-ba-bang!" He could keep firing as long as he could keep shouting it.

For the man, it was hard to relate to that avid and active imagination. The wide mustard field was too peaceful for a bloody battlefield, and the beauty of the shining sun was making him lazy and sleepy. Even so, he held his bamboo stick and hobbled along with the boy.

"Landmine. Get down!" shouted the boy.

Hearing the order, the man sluggishly fell on the ground. He didn't mind getting some dirt on his clothes as they were shabby to begin with. But he was already in his mid-thirties—too old to run around with a bamboo stick like a boy. He had a dark, chiseled face with a prominent hooked nose, and his timid eyes were watching the boy.

"Commanding Officer," said the boy with a serious look as he lay flat in a depression behind a small rise of higher ground.

"What do you want?" said the man.

"You shouldn't say 'What do you want,'" said the boy. "We are in combat."

"In combat," the man murmured, and he put on a grave expression as if he were convinced.

"Ba-boom!" the boy shouted. "That was surely a howitzer."

"Could've been a mortar," the man mumbled.

"No chance," the boy argued. "That was a twelve-inch howitzer."

"Well, maybe so," the man said unconvincingly.

"Commanding Officer!" the boy said again. "The enemy's attack is so fierce. If we do nothing and this continues, we are just waiting to be annihilated."

"What? Annihilated?" the man said.

"Yes, annihilated," the boy repeated. "Commanding Officer, work out a plan of attack quickly."

"Well," said the man, "what should we do?"

"How about outflanking the enemy troops on the left side …" the boy suggested.

"Outflanking," the man mumbled sorrowfully, surveying the expanse of golden flowers. He couldn't bear the thought of crawling around the large plantation. His joints were hurting and his knees still painful from when he had fallen to the ground on the boy's orders.

"Outflanking is no good," he announced with authority.

"Then," said the boy, "let's send in a suicide corps."

"Suicide corps?" he asked back anxiously. "What are they supposed to do?"

"Make a dash from here," said the boy, "and dive into the enemy's bunkers with explosives."

"I see, make a dash," said the man to himself. "But we don't have explosives, do we?"

The boy looked around quickly and saw a long, thick tree trunk half-buried in the field.

"There's one," he excitedly said, "let's use that. It looks like the bomb that Three Brave Bullet Soldiers carried.[1] Commanding Officer, what do you think?"

The log the boy dragged to him was half-rotten, and he would get sticky sap on his hand and maybe splinters if he touched it.

"Suicide corps won't work, either," he hurriedly said.

"Why not?"

"Our loss would be too big."

"But we are prepared to die."

"No matter what, it's no good."

"Then, what shall we do?"

"Let's retreat. It's over."

Standing up slowly, the man rubbed his back and beat the dirt off his pants and shirt. Then he rubbed a hand over his face and shook his head a couple of times, as if sending a signal that it was, in fact, fin-

---

1 "Three Brave Bullet Soldiers" (*bakudan sanyūshi* 爆弾三勇士)—Eshita Takeji 江下武二, Kitagawa Susumu 北川丞, and Sakue Inosuke 作江伊之助—died during the 1932 Shanghai Incident, carrying a bomb and breaking through the line of a Chinese encampment.

ished. His countenance showed the reason and will of a mature man. He had had enough of this childish game and was going back to work.

The boy resented the man's reluctance to continue.

"Oh, damn," he pouted. "It's not fair."

"I quit," the man said flatly. "I cannot play with you any longer."

"Tadpoles," the boy said. "You're going to feed your tadpoles, aren't you?"

"Yes," answered the man, "and other business."

"But you promised," the boy said, "that we would play the game until we occupied the oak woods."

"I don't care about the woods," the man replied.

"Then," the boy said in a threatening tone, "I don't care to go catch tadpoles next Sunday."

"All right," said the man, "don't go if you don't want to."

Suddenly, however, he had an unsettling feeling. He knew he was the least important member of the family. He was still single, had no job, and was a burden to his older brother. Even his brother's three young sons looked down on him, although they used him as their playmate. He secretly had a plan to grow edible frogs on a grand scale, but so far all he could do with the little money he had was to catch tadpoles from a marsh in Chiba Prefecture with the help of his brother's children and keep them in several fish tanks, experimenting with ways to grow them faster and larger. The truth is, though he called it an experiment, it was more like idle child's play. The word "tadpoles" didn't exactly sound important, so his mother, his older brother, and his brother's wife scoffed at his venture. His tadpoles made everyone view this already incompetent man as a complete fool.

It would be a severe blow if the children decided not to help him. The children already knew his situation.

Knowing his uncle's predicament, the boy said, "If I don't go, the catch will be much smaller."

The man growled.

"I can catch twice as many as Shigeru does," the boy said.

"You're right," he admitted.

"I would like to help you," the boy said. "If we occupy the oak woods, I'd catch thirty tadpoles."

"Hmmm," the man nodded, feeling manipulated.

"I'll bring a four-armed scoop net," the boy continued shrewdly, "then I'll be able to catch fifty ..."

"All right," the man said hurriedly. "I should occupy that place over there, right?"

"Yep," said the boy shrewdly.

"It's just that," the man pleaded, "you shouldn't try catching carp but focus on catching only tadpoles that will grow to be edible frogs."

"Yeah, yeah," replied the boy.

"And bring them home carefully so they don't die. You know, the last time ..."

"I know, Uncle," the boy snapped. Changing his tone now he said, "Commanding Officer, shall we send in a suicide corps?"

"Fine," the man sighed. "We have no other choice."

"Who'll we send?" the boy asked excitedly.

"Major Kijima!" the man called.

"Yes, sir."

"Come with me."

"Yes, sir!"

The boy sprang to his feet like a cat, grabbed the old log, and prepared to make his heroic attack. The man reluctantly picked up the other end of the bomb, cringing as he felt the clammy soil and slimy wood in his hands.

The boy started his advance, building up his speed until he was running hard, trampling mustard flowers in the process. The man tried to keep up though he ran awkwardly with his long legs and hunched back over the soft, uneven soil.

Soon, a small and a large figure, carrying the decayed log between them, rushed into the oak woods, the small figure shouting a manly war whoop, the large one letting out a whining moan.

Soon again, a real war began. It rapidly and incessantly evolved from a little war into a large one.

The man and the boy joined the real war in reverse order. The boy departed as the first student sent to the front, and died in the South Pacific in spectacular fashion. The man was drafted toward the end of the war as a lesser recruit, and wandered aimlessly about inland China, lost and weak, until he succumbed to malnutrition.

It was no different from the way they had played their war game so long ago.

■■■

death

Shi

死

In February 1953, I was in practical training as an intern at a university hospital in Sendai. The training was nearing its end, so I could be as lazy as I wanted. I was more concerned about the national medical exam that was coming up in April.

I knew that a majority of those who took the medical exam would pass so it would be shameful and humiliating if I failed. Nevertheless I could not motivate myself to study. Others appeared to feel the same way.

Medical college students study for a year longer than students in other colleges. After that, we have to spend a year as interns and then take the national medical exam. At this point, we were tired and had had enough of exams.

In this frame of mind, many of my fellow students were more into drinking than studying. Thinking back, we all drank too much, even though we were students. We would first go to a big liquor store near Sendai Station. In those days, a liquor store had tables and chairs and served alcohol by the glass. The store was right in front of a big cabaret, and soldiers from the American base would drink whisky straight out of a small bottle. Some people who went to the cabaret were stingy enough to get half-drunk on cheap liquor beforehand at the liquor store. Then we would go to a small tavern in Higashi Ichiban-chō. We also went to a bar to look for acquaintances we knew from the tavern, and they often bought us drinks, knowing we were needy students. We drank a lot by exhausting our credit or by scrounging from others.

At that time, I dreamed quite often. I read books on dreams by Freud and Ellis, and since I was interested in dreams and planning to go into psychiatry, I was thinking of doing some research on dreams. Therefore I wrote down my own dreams, one after another. The more I grew accustomed to doing it, the more detail I could record. When I would wake up in the middle of the night, I would immediately turn on the light and write down my dream in a notebook beside my pillow. Some nights when I had a nightmare, my intestines would make weird noises, and I was modestly excited that Ellis described the same phenomenon.

The dreams that I had written down varied greatly, but many concerned sexual desire, directly or indirectly. I was at that stage in my life then.

Here I quote three of my dreams recorded in the notebook:

> The dream I had at dawn: The girl *I* from Motokazuhira is in the room and she kisses me. The feeling of her teeth biting my tongue is so real. Then my older brother comes in (she hears his footsteps but does not let go of my tongue) and asks me to help with his patient. I leave and when I come back to the room, there is a note she left saying something like she doesn't want to submit herself to me.

> I am riding on a bus or a train. I have a gun in my hand. I am upset because a man is stopping me from sitting on a seat, then I realize that it is actually my gun being stuck that makes me unable to sit down. A woman is looking at my gun suspiciously. I get off at the station near my house, and a female conductor runs after me, accusing me of giving her a fake or stolen ticket. I get upset and suggest that we go to the police station or anywhere she wants. Before I know it, we are in front of a dining hall in a department store. She and I are no longer upset with each other. Before going to the police station,

> I suggest, "Let's eat something." I intend to treat her, but she quickly purchases dining tickets. I look at them and see they are for a full meal. I don't want her to spend money on me, so I tell her that just coffee or tea will do, and I have her return the tickets. Our two cups of tea cost only 40 yen, and the salesperson looks disappointed.

There were more intense dreams:

> I kill a baby. There are spots, one between the ribs and one a bit lower, where inserting a scalpel will kill a baby instantly. But I forget where those spots are, and the baby does not die easily. Having no alternative, I cut him again and again, and cut his intestines into pieces. He cries with a distorted face, and I get scared. Soon a police officer arrives to investigate, and he finds drops of blood on tatami mats or a carpet on the floor. I am resigned, knowing that I will be arrested ...

If I force myself to analyze this dream, it appears to stem from a time when I was about to sleep with a woman but decided not to since she said it was the time of month when it was easy to get pregnant.

I was spending my days being slovenly, drinking heavily, having sex dreams, and not studying much for the medical exam.

On February 25, I came back to my boarding house at around four o'clock in the morning, completely drunk, with my friend Mr. Shinoi. Mr. Shinoi was one year my senior in high school. Back then, he was in the track and field club, tirelessly running on the athletic field all the time. That's why his face was familiar to me. I met Mr. Shinoi by chance when I was on the train with a few friends on our way to take the entrance examination at the university in Sendai. Having failed to enter medical school the previous year, he'd waited for another chance to enroll and was heading to Sendai to take the exam again. My friends and I felt strongly that we must do better than he who had failed the exam the previous year. Whenever our conversation touched on subjects in the exam, he said, "I don't know about this subject" and opened his book in a hurry. He seemed good-natured but rather helpless.

Fortunately both Mr. Shinoi and I passed the exam. We became classmates at medical school, but he was still our senior when it came to drinking and most everything else, so we called him "Mr." and somehow regarded him as our leader.

For a while Mr. Shinoi lived with a woman who worked in a bar, and then he dumped her. I envied him his worldliness and showed him respect.

That February evening, or rather, early morning, I had been drinking heavily with Mr. Shinoi and, since his boarding house was further away, we came back to mine and squeezed onto one futon.

I had various dreams then, which included one about my father. I was visiting somewhere in the countryside, and we appeared to be at a gathering hosted by an admirer of my father. My father, the poet Saitō Mokichi, was advanced in years. When I had been home in Tokyo that winter break, he was already becoming senile so I was expecting that he would not be with us for long. In all my recorded dreams, my father never appeared, but in this ambiguous dream, he was surely there. I don't remember whether he appeared physically but I felt his presence there.

In the morning, a telegram arrived. My room was on the second floor and near the top of the stairs so I clearly heard the man's voice calling out "Telegram!" Instantly, I had a flash that my father had died. It startled me in spite of my hangover. But the telegram was addressed to Watanabe, my landlord, so I went back to sleep.

Early that afternoon I heard another telegram being delivered but assumed it too was for Watanabe, so I didn't bother to get up. The elderly landlady seemed to be out, so half-awake and half-asleep, I heard Mr. Shinoi get up and go downstairs. Then I heard the man at the door say, "Saitō Sōkichi." Saitō Sōkichi is my name. I was startled and sat up in bed, and soon Mr. Shinoi brought me the telegram. It was from Tokyo. "It has finally come," I thought. When I opened the telegram, I saw: "Father in critical condition. Come home soon. Shigeta." Shigeta is my older brother.

What I was thinking or how I was feeling then—I have no recollection. Hurriedly I checked the timetable for trains to Tokyo, but unfortunately there were none until that night. Mr. Shinoi saw that I was at a loss and urged me to call home. Since there was no telephone in my boarding house, I used the phone in the house across the street. The call went through within fifteen minutes, and Shigeta picked up the phone. "How is he?" I asked. My brother, also a doctor, said one word: "*Gestorben* (died)."

Suddenly the tears came, and my voice trembled uncontrollably. I couldn't help it. It was a sudden upheaval of emotion that I did not expect. As I called the telephone company to check the fee for the call, my tears flowed ceaselessly, and I was ashamed.

I returned to the boarding house and had a late lunch with Mr. Shinoi. Soon I started to calm down and even told some jokes.

My father's death was timely and unsurprising. His brain had stopped working long ago while his body hung on in a frail, geriatric state that was painful to see. The father that I had known ever since I could remember had long left this world.

After the war, in Ōishida, where he had moved for safety from the U.S. bombing raids, my father suffered from pleurisy. His body began to decline quickly after that. By 1949, he started to have difficulty walking and he became partially paralyzed on his left side. He had his first heart attack in February 1951, and in April of the following year he had two consecutive serious attacks. His breathing was shallow and rapid, and cyanosis[1] appeared on his lips, hands, and feet, but he managed to survive.

Considering his age and previous illnesses, such a physical decline would have been inevitable. However, along with his physical decline was his mental deterioration. More plainly speaking, his brain was damaged. He gradually developed senile dementia that was probably caused by hardening of the arteries in his brain over a period of time—a cruel physiological aspect of aging with no cure.

When I was home in October of the previous year, I saw him in such a condition. If nobody was around, he would get up from his bed and bang on the door shouting, "Hey, hey!" I supported him when he

1. Cyanosis is an abnormal bluish discoloration of the skin.

walked, but he yelled "Ouch, ouch!" so loudly that it caught me off guard. He was no longer able to speak a long word clearly. He would be helped to a dining room chair, then to a rattan chair in his room, and then onto his futon, but he was never comfortable, and he would yell, "Hey, hey!" in a beastlike tone so that someone would help him up again. He was so decrepit that when he said anything like "Thank you," such as when I helped him sit in a chair then put a blanket on his lap, his words took me by surprise.

One day I found him repeating the words "… inferior, inferior …," but he was unable to say the rest. I imagined that he was trying to say he was an inferior creature.

When I went home on New Year's Day this year, my father's condition had worsened and he could no longer walk. We would help him sit in a chair and feed him his meals, but he sometimes tried to eat with his fingers. He'd peel an orange with his trembling hands and put the peel in his mouth. When he saw me, he showed almost no reaction, whereas earlier when I went home during school breaks he was always happy to see me.

He became incontinent. He was incapable of telling others when he wanted to urinate. After he wet the bed, he would call to us, "Hey, hey." Not surprisingly, there was a strong odor of urine around him. When we put him down on the futon, he sometimes rolled off it. He constantly made his beastly cry, "Hey, hey." I thought of the horrible death of Chamberlain Christoph Detlev Brigge, who screamed and groaned in Rilke's *The Notebooks of Malte Laurids Brigge.*[2] When we went near our father, he grabbed our arms. His fingers held quite a bit of strength, so it was painful when he clutched my arm. He could no longer speak a comprehensible word. To put it bluntly, he was completely demented.

I looked at him with mixed feelings. Nothing remained of his former self. He seemed a living corpse rather than a feeble old body. Compared to other family members who had to take care of him constantly, I had it easy: after a few days there I could return to Sendai. I

---

2. *The Notebooks of Malte Laurids Brigge* (*Die Aufzeichnungen des Malte Laurids Brigge*) by Rainer Maria Rilke (1875–1926) was published in 1910.

found it painful to look at him. Perhaps I should have spent more time with him while I was at home during vacations but I never did. I always had excuses to leave the house with errands to run.

According to the Complete Collection of my father's works, there are only twelve poems written by him in 1952, the year before his death. However, we cannot be certain that even these small number of poems were all actually written then. One thing for sure is that he did not compose much poetry that year.

Among the twelve poems is this one:

Before I realized
the sun has set;
in this world
now I live, but
my end, too, is probably near[3]

According to my mother, he wrote this poem without anyone noticing on a piece of paper at his bedside. Certainly this is about the last poem he composed, although in his collection of works the following poem is listed at the end:

In my mouth
I taste only bitterness,
but I ignore it
as I try to sleep
in my bedroom in the daytime[4]

---

3. The original poem reads:

itsushika mo	いつしかも
hi ga shizumi yuki	日がしづみゆき
utsusemi no	うつせみの
ware mo onozukara	われもおのづから
kiwamaru rashi mo	きはまるらしも

4 The original poem reads:

kuchinaka ga	口中が
mohara nigaki mo	専ら苦きも
kaerimizu	かえりみず
hiru no fushido ni	晝のふしどに
nemuramu to suru	ねむらむとする

These must have been composed by early summer at the latest. When my father could no longer write poetry, his health declined very rapidly. By New Year's Day 1953 he was in miserable shape, as I mentioned earlier.

Then, in the early afternoon of February 25, I was informed of his death. I admit that receiving the news while I was hung over was disgraceful, but his death happened when it was intended to happen—or so I thought once I had calmed down.

I had one distant relative in Sendai, and I went out to mail him a letter saying I would be going to Tokyo on that evening's train. It was cold, and the sky was overcast and wintry, with translucent light suffusing the area. Only the clamor of children's voices could be heard. Next to the mailbox was a dog, and when I held out my hand to him, he pressed his icy-cold nose into my palm. In a nearby normal school, workers were tearing out broken glass from the windows and dropping it to the ground. The clatter of glass falling on the ground resounded sharply.

I had nothing to do until the evening train, so I lay down on the bed. It seemed that my sadness had lifted, but I still felt hollow and empty as I kept thinking that my father was gone, he was no more in this world.

The seven o'clock news on the radio reported my father's death. I was having dinner with people in my boarding house, and I felt as if this news report was about someone else, not the father I had known.

I got on the 8:20 express train, and even though it was an express train, I would not arrive in Tokyo until early the next morning. I have never been good at sleeping on trains. While being jolted all night, I watched tiny water droplets gathering on the window. When the train stopped at one station, I saw a street behind the platform, shining as if it were wet. At another station, I got off and stood around on the platform since our train had a long wait for another train. A cold, light drizzle was falling.

As the midnight train gently rocked me as it went along the tracks,

I thought about my father vaguely as if it were all something that had happened in a faraway world.

Ever since I was a child, I thought of my father as short-tempered, for he often got angry, clicking his tongue and trembling with rage. I could never get used to his anger; hearing him become angry with anyone always scared me.

I remember the time a guest showed up at our door. He appeared to be a member of the Araragi school of poetry who had come to Tokyo from the countryside. The maid told him that my father, the master, was lying down with a cold, but he insisted on seeing the master face to face since he had taken the trouble to travel a long distance. A while after the maid went upstairs, my father rushed down, making a big noise that can be only described as "impulsive impudence," a phrase my father often used in his poetry. He exploded with anger: "I really do have a cold and I was resting—you think I'm lying?" In such cases, he always ranted on and on for several minutes. I was just a schoolchild at the time and was so terrified that my body shrank as I listened to his outburst behind the paper screen between rooms.

When my father got angry, he always did so with all his body and soul, and it was generally directed toward someone he was familiar with, such as a family member or a close disciple. His anger could be ignited over any matter, even the most trivial things.

He once wrote an essay about a rude interpreter he encountered when he was trying to move a Western patient to another hospital:

> ... The head nurse in my branch hospital was conferring with the interpreter who was staying at the hotel. In a supplicating tone, the head nurse was asking him to transfer the patient to another hospital. I did not know what he was saying to her, but their conversation did not seem to go anywhere. So I took the phone and told him again about transferring her. To my surprise, he rudely said, "What's this about?" and "When did I promise you such a thing?" I was burning mad and was unrelenting, and I immediately chastised him for his language, and ordered the hospital director to transfer the patient to M Hospital.

As he had written in that essay, when he was "burning mad," he became "unrelenting" and had to "chastise" someone. It was like a war or a battle. To those who were subjected to his anger, it was truly intolerable.

When I was in middle school, I received a bad grade in English dictation. I didn't have to show it to him, but I let him see it without thinking. He flared up and told me to bring him the English textbook right away and he made me take dictation from him. My father was extremely busy and usually didn't have time to play with his children, but this time he gave me the exercise for nearly an hour. I was gripped with fear the entire time.

Although my father was scary, he loved his children. However, his affection arose from his own ego and his strong personality, and his suffocating attentions were an unwelcome favor. Frankly speaking, he was more concerned with his sons than his daughters, and he favored those of us who did better in school. I did well in elementary and middle schools so I would say I got a lot of affection from him. However, until I graduated from middle school, I saw no benefit in having such a frightening father.

My older brother and older and younger sisters liked our mother more than our father. She had separated from him when I was little, and she lived with my uncle in the main family house. It was not until the spring of 1945 that our mother was allowed to come home. Until then, we secretly went to our uncle's house on Sundays to visit her. Seeing her only occasionally, she seemed very kind, and our visits were wonderful. As a matter of fact, our mother also had a strong personality, which surely had contributed to their breakup: two self-assertive people can rarely get along. At any rate, we children did not understand such subtle human interactions, so we all bore a feeling like a grudge against our father for kicking our mother out of the house.

It seemed as though our father was so busy that he tacitly permitted us to go see her. Once, when he asked me where I had been, I told him a fib and I somewhat remember that he severely scolded me for being a liar. His anger might have been something similar to the sentiment expressed in this poem of his:

Pitiful, oh, pitiful,
like a flashing light
I enrage;
there are times when
I hate even my own children.[5]

Our father would show his children affection in his own way, but there is no doubt that he was also a tyrannical father.

When I learned to play Japanese chess[6] in elementary school, he was amused and rather delighted. However, when I became so enthusiastic about it that I clipped game charts from the newspaper and he began to lose against me, he told me I should not play it anymore.

My father was rather unskilled at Japanese chess. He was impulsive at the chessboard. He recklessly took the offensive by placing a rook at the center position and then moving both silver generals.[7] If he succeeded in breaking through the opponent's central line, he would win by a wide margin, but if his opponent mounted any defense, it was the end for him. He was unyielding and he hated to lose, so when he got trounced by Kōda Rohan,[8] he bought a book on chess tactics at a night stall and studied some moves with me.

He prohibited me from playing chess by saying, "Devote yourself to studying. Once you get into college, you can take lessons and if you study under a master you'll soon be in the senior class."

But that promise was a total lie. After I entered college, he never allowed me to take chess lessons; he simply told me to study more diligently.

Being forbidden from playing chess wasn't the worst of it; I was totally shocked to be stopped from collecting insects. I had begun col-

---

5. The original poem reads:

aware aware	あはれあはれ
den no gotoku ni	電のごとくに
hiramekite	ひらめきて
waga kora sura o	わが子等すらを
nikumu koto ari	にくむことあり

6. The word for Japanese chess used in the original text is *shōgi*.
7. The Japanese game has two silver and two gold generals.
8. Kōda Rohan 幸田露伴 (1867–1947) was a novelist.

lecting insects in elementary school, and in the second or the third year of middle school, I became obsessed with the desire to become an entomologist. Not being allowed to subscribe to the newsletter of an amateur insect-collectors' club, I asked a driver from the hospital to subscribe to it for me under his name, but my father caught on to this and both the driver and I were sternly reproached. I don't believe collecting insects is a bad hobby, but my father never allowed me to do anything that might interrupt my studies. He constantly insisted that I study. In my desk drawer I had hidden some books that were not related to school subjects, and as soon as I heard his footsteps coming—fortunately, they made a distinctive sound—I would instantly shut the drawer.

He often asked me about the result of school tests in his own dictatorial way: "Could you answer everything correctly?" If I said, "All except one," he impatiently pressed me harder, asking, "Why not? Why couldn't you do it?"

There was of course nothing I could do about the fact that I hadn't answered everything correctly, but he couldn't understand that and kept grumbling over and over. I could not help but think that I was unlucky to have such father.

In my fourth year at middle school when I failed the entrance exam to a high school, my father spent a long time being upset and kept on unreasonably castigating me. I had passed the secondary exam for Tokyo University Special School of Medicine, which existed during the war. However, I yearned for the white-lined cap worn by high school students, so I was planning on taking the entrance exam again. With another year left in middle school, I still had time; it wasn't as though I would lose out on having a school to go to. But since the war was going badly, my father thought I should enter the Special School of Medicine right away lest I get drafted before entering high school. As always, he fretted over the problem too much to make a decision himself so he took me all the way to Professor Hirafuku Ichirō in the Department of Pathology at Tokyo University to consult with him. On the way back, he mulled it over more and more, and finally ordered me to go to the Special School of Medicine, whether I wanted to or not. When I sadly nodded in agreement to my father, he suddenly warmed to me and bought me an expensive academic picture book of insects.

Three days after I started at the Special School of Medicine, he summoned me and asked, "Sōkichi, how old are you?"

"I'm nineteen."

"Nineteen? Then I made a calculation error—you won't be drafted. How would you like to try getting into high school again?"

So I ended up going back for my fifth year of middle school. I understood that he was concerned about me, but I couldn't help but think that he was very oppressive and selfish. I spent my days in fear of him, felt uncomfortable in his presence, and even held grudges against him. This, however, changed dramatically in 1945, the year the war ended.

Thinking back on it now, it had been a frantic year. I passed the entrance exam to Matsumoto High School but I was working in a factory where middle-school students had been mobilized. In April, my father moved to Yamagata Prefecture for safety. Later, my factory burned down. At the end of May, my house also burned down. I left home for the first time in my life and went to Matsumoto. These upheavals affected me greatly, and I was also in spiritual puberty at that time. At the home of my relatives', where I stayed after my house was destroyed, I found my father's poetry books. They gave me one of them, *Cold Cloud,* so I took it with me to Shinshū.[9]

I had seldom read literary books and had never read my father's poetry. On my father's bookshelf, I once saw his book *Nagatsuka Takashi,* but I misread the title as *Nagatsuka bushi* and thought he was not only a poet but also a scholar of folk ballads.[10]

---

9. Shinshū is the traditional name for Nagano Prefecture. Matsumoto High School, which Kita Morio attended and is now Shinshū University, is located in Nagano Prefecture.

10. Nagatsuka Takashi 長塚節 (1879–1915) was a poet and novelist. The Kanji character for "Takashi" 節 can also be read as "fushi/bushi," which means "melody" and

The war was going against Japan more and more each day. In Matsumoto, B-29s often flew over in formation to drop mines on the port in Niigata. There was a secret military project in a camouflaged commerce-school building that stood across the school grounds from the dormitory, where they kept experimenting with a rocket engine. We could hear roaring sounds and see billows of white smoke. But for the most part the town of Matsumoto seemed very quiet in contrast with the Tokyo I had fled, which was covered with debris and ashes. At night in Matsumoto, all I heard were frogs calling in the nearby rice paddies. It was my first experience hearing the clamorous, indescribable voices of frogs. It was precisely as written in the poem, "I hear the call of frogs in distant paddies echoing in the sky."[11]

I read my father's poems with strong feelings. I am ashamed to write this, but for the first time in my life I trembled as I read. It was probably the sentimentality of adolescence, but the image of my father that I had retained for so many years now suddenly and drastically changed: He was no longer frightening and unbearable, he was transformed into the poet named Mokichi. I obtained his book *Morning Fireflies,* a collection of his own choosing, and read it avidly. It really spoke to me because its poems mentioned places I was familiar with as a child, such as the Aoyama Cemetery in my neighborhood and the mental hospital—I disliked the fact that I had been born there. Before long, I became a fan, or a worshipper, of Mokichi.

In July before the end of the war, our dormitory was closed, so I went to Yamagata where my father had been evacuated. On the way, I felt strange and even humbled. However, upon arriving there after

---

is often used in titles of Japanese traditional folk ballads, such as Shōnai-bushi 庄内節, Sōran-bushi ソーラン節, or Tankō-bushi 炭坑節.

11. The phrase is part of a poem composed by Saitō Mokichi, which reads:

shi ni chikaki	死に近き
haha ni soine no	母に添寝の
shinshin to	しんしんと
tōta no kawazu	遠田のかはづ
ten ni kikoyuru	天に聞こゆる

I lie next to / my mother who is near her death. / As evening wears on / I hear the call of frogs in distant paddies / echoing in the sky.

making my difficult trip near the end of the war, I found my father once again angrily rebuking my mother in very harsh tones. She was staying there because our house in Tokyo had burned, and he was constantly infuriated by trivial matters. Most of all, he was infuriated by fleas. I did better with the Mokichi of his books; in real life I felt suffocated when I was around him for a long time. Even so, when he went out for a walk, I took out his poetry collections *Red Light* and *Unpolished Gem* and copied some of the poems in my little notebook.

When I later attended school in the provinces, the further away I got from him, the more my secret admiration for him grew. From college in Sendai, I went home for every vacation, thinking that, since he was getting older, I should show him more devotion before it was too late. But again, the more days I spent with him, the more oppressed I felt by his strong self-assertiveness, and the more eager I was to go back to Sendai as soon as possible.

For instance, my father strictly prohibited me from smoking. He told me that when he was young he had smoked "until the smoke came out of his behind." Then he quit for health reasons and he forced his new beliefs on his sons. One day late at night, when I figured he was asleep, I lit a cigarette in the room next to his bedroom. Before I had inhaled once or twice, his angry voice pierced through the paper screen door: "Hey Sōkichi, are you smoking?" He had animalistic instincts about such things.

I spent one summer vacation alone with my father in a cottage next to our main summerhouse in Hakone. We lived in only two rooms, which was very stressful. I was in charge of cooking, plus he had me mow the lawn, clear leaves from the gutter, and clean the rooms. During all these chores, he would stand right next to me, supervising and instructing and clicking his tongue. He couldn't bear to entrust things to others because he wanted everything done his way.

For the first half of the vacation, I was happy and honored to spend time with my father, but to be honest, during the last half I became really sick of him. Most of the time I had to read secretly if my books were not about medicine, and I had to sneak into the woods two or three times a day, huddling under an umbrella when it rained, just to smoke a cigarette.

When I was cleaning his room, I did enjoy stealing glances at the notebook he left on his desk. He used to study very vigorously every summer, but his compositions were declining as he grew older. I was delighted to come upon a good poem in his notebook once in a while, but when I saw the mediocre ones they made me think: "Mokichi has gotten old." That summer, he composed very little, worrying instead about the people who were renting the main summerhouse, or about bugs that had bred in his bamboo wicker trunk. Occasionally he quizzed me on medicine and if I could not answer, he clicked his tongue and got upset, saying, "I studied this decades ago and I remember it. How can you now be a medical student and not know it?"

After the trials of that vacation were over, I went back to my college in a provincial city. When I was away from my father I, again, experienced a longing for him. I loved my father and I despised my father. This continued for a number of years, and unfortunately, I never once showed him the devotion in a way my heart would have desired.

I arrived at Ueno Station at 5:20 A.M. and changed to a local train. The sky began dimming around Ikebukuro. When I exited Shinjuku Station, a misty rain was falling. I took a taxi and arrived home at around 6:00 A.M.

Because my family did not conduct a wake, it was very quiet at home. My younger sister was up and took me to my father's room. My mother appeared to be sleeping in the next room and did not come out to see me. My father's corpse was laid out under a silk coverlet. He used to sleep under an older one, but now a beautiful spread covered him. His body would never move again.

The moment I removed the cloth from his face and looked down at him I was startled by his skinny, pale, sharp face. His beard (which a nurse had shaved a few days earlier) was sparse, and there was still a little swelling around his mouth. His cheekbones protruded slightly, and his closed eyes seemed narrow and small. His short eyelashes contrasted with his bushy eyebrows. As I observed him for a while, his face, with his mouth slightly open, was the sleeping face I was familiar with, but obviously he belonged to the hard world of death. I heard my younger sister sobbing behind me. There was no other sound in the room, and it felt very cold.

I went to the dining room and drank tea, then went back to the room where my father lay, this time by myself. I felt a certain happiness at being able to view his face as much as I wanted to without being interrupted by anyone. I lifted the coverlet and touched his skinny feet. Then I traced his face with my fingers.

His large earlobes had not yet become stiff. His cheeks and forehead were cold to the touch. Underneath the light gray wool socks, his ankles were already rigid and could not be moved, and the skin just above his shinbones was as cold as ice. The hands joined together on his chest were also too stiff to move. His wrists were not as cold and almost felt as if a pulse were still beating there. I spent quite some time looking at my father and touching his body.

At eight o'clock a eulogy was given by Yūki Aisōka,[12] and a recording of my father reciting his own poems was broadcast on the radio. The recording had been made many years earlier and featured several of his poems, including this one:

As evening deepens,
on radish leaves
winter rain falls;
In extreme loneliness,
ah, it's drizzling[13]

---

12. Yūki Aisōka 結城哀草果 (1893–1974) was a poet and essayist who studied poetry under Saitō Mokichi.

13. The original poem reads:

yū sareba	ゆふされば
daikon no ha ni	大根の葉に
furu shigure	ふるしぐれ
itaku sabishiku	いたく寂しく
furinikeru kamo	降りにけるかも

The way he recited his poems was faltering; he recited the third verse in complete isolation, adding the fifth verse again in isolation. As the broadcast was ending, the people who were to assist us started to arrive, and it was getting crowded in the house.

Only once in my life had I wanted to assert my own will in the face of my father's disagreement. In a letter (it was impossible to express my own will directly to his face), I told him thatI wanted to study zoology in college. He must have been shocked to hear that. He replied in a letter that began with polite language:

> I fully sympathize with your love for zoology, Sōkichi. I also loved zoology during my boyhood and adolescent years.
>
> By the way, if you do major in zoology, how will you make a living after graduation? Let's suppose you work at a college as a research assistant for very little money; after that, would you become a teacher? Or are you going to be a technical expert somewhere? How do zoologists make their living now? That is what I, as your father, would most like to know and am concerned about. I think they probably don't lead a comfortable life and they feel anxious about starting a family.
>
> If it were peacetime, I would have planned for Shigeta too to engage in research and get his degree, but that was not possible after the defeat in the war. There seems to be no future in psychiatry, so I have been lying awake at night thinking you should instead major in surgery and set up in a hospital independent from Shigeta. If you major in surgery, I believe you can make a living and feed your family. Even if you were only an assistant at a college, you could make enough. That is what I wish for you. If you went into zoology, things would turn out quite contrary to my expectations for you, and I am afraid that your life would be difficult.
>
> In middle school, students usually follow their parents' opinion about studying as they do not have any of their own. In high school, however, their own thoughts about studying begin to sprout, and considering their aptitudes and other things, they become idealistic. Probably almost 100 percent of high school students feel the same way. So you are not alone, Sōkichi. But in reality, it is very difficult

to realize one's ideals, and many people live ordinary and unpleasant lives. "Idealism," therefore, is ordinary and immature, a mere sentiment of adolescence. What I would like you to do is to look seriously at the hard, present reality (*gegenwärtige Wirklichkeit*). I would like you to face squarely Japan's defeat and the current situation of our family (especially the problems of tuition and the cost of living). (a) Zoology is similar to basic medicine, so I'm afraid it will not bring you enough money and that you will spend all your life being a teacher; (b) Currently Shigeta, with seven people in his family, is constantly in debt. He barely supports his family using royalties from my books. I am already advanced in life. I have reached the state of an "old body left behind."

I am sending you this letter with my infinite love for you. Upon examining and clearly considering things, write me a reply as soon as possible. It has been the case that your letters do not respond to my questions, so pay special attention to answer my questions in your letter.

Also, it must be inconvenient to study if you live in a boarding house that is far from school. Tell me honestly and immediately what your current grade average is and where you stand among your classmates after the test in the second semester.

I am not planning to forcibly deny your will, but things must be carefully considered over and over again. Therefore respond to me quickly. In the field of medicine, surgery seems to be the most enjoyable subject as clinical practice (*praktische Medizin*). What is your opinion on this? There are many people who wish to change their majors from zoology to medicine, but few who wish it the other way around. (I'm telling you this as a practical matter.)

You must have been saddened by my previous letter. That is totally understandable. You think that what I told you goes against your desires and aptitudes.

Enclosed are comprehensive comments from zoology majors at Tokyo Imperial University, so they are very relevant to you. Please read them calmly. They seem to have no concern about earning a living, which is not the case for you. It would be very difficult for you to show your true worth if you majored in zoology.

Let's talk thoroughly when you come back to Tokyo this winter vacation. Until then, please study with all your might.

Subsequent letters became harsher in tone.

The reason I encouraged you to live in the dorm is because I thought it would be more convenient for you to study. On the contrary, it turned out to harm you. It was my mistake, and I cannot regret it more. It's a shame that you were compelled to become a committee member.

I am writing this after careful consideration and asking others' opinions. Stating my conclusion first, I still want you to become a medical doctor. Please make a concerted effort in this direction as you have been doing. This is a request from your elderly father. A parent-child relationship is pure, and there is no way that I can sit back and watch you as a spectator. A parent's love for a child is also genuine. I can imagine how you will be grateful for my advice when you turn forty, but if you go against it and became a zoologist, limiting yourself to teaching, how will you feel? My concern is purely my love for my child.

Recently, Professor Miyaji wrote me and informed me of your grades. You are twenty-sixth out of forty-two students, and you are especially bad at mathematics and physics. At this level, it will be impossible for you to enter medical school at Tokyo University.

Sōkichi, you were an excellent scholar as a child and an honor student throughout elementary and middle school. So why are you not excelling in high school, when it is so important? It is because you have become stupid. You have been enjoying an idealistic, arrogant outlook and are not fully conscious of the realities of life. I warned you again and again about this, but you did not heed my advice. It is not too late: wake up as soon as you read this letter and throw insects out of your life, and study as hard as you can. Get credit as the excellent student you have been. High school is the place where you should fully awaken. How stupid you are to spend time and energy collecting insects!

I would be greatly saddened if you have not determined to go into medicine and continue procrastinating about your studies. I was disappointed when I saw your exam grades this September (and

I suspect some professors graded you quite sympathetically, so your actual learning may have been even lower). I'm concerned about your entrance exam next spring. For zoology or botany, a weak-minded person could get in without taking an exam. Not so for medicine, especially at Tokyo University. That is why students are studying so hard to get in. At this most important time, you should not be concerned about Danaid eggflies[14] or Jean-Henri Fabre.[15] You were an excellent student before you got into Matsumoto High School, and then you were flustered and became stupid. How awful this is!

Even a medical doctor cannot make a living as easily as before. He has to make a great effort. Shigeta is struggling more than I could have imagined.

But medicine is an interesting field. You are interested in zoology and botany only because you do not know how interesting medicine is. If you study medicine, you will find it very complex and deep. The study of medicine includes many other subjects, including zoology and botany.

Burn this letter about your aspirations. Also, respond to this letter immediately.

Put all your efforts into studying the subjects on the entrance exam, such as physics, mathematics, chemistry, German, and others. If any student come to visit you at your boarding house, immediately send them away. Do not be defeated by your idealism or by being flattered. This is your father's utmost order.

I have written the above in a state of frustration, so forgive me.

It's no wonder I gave up on going into zoology. I didn't have the nerve to go against my father's wishes after receiving letters like these.

At around nine thirty in the morning, a Buddhist monk chanted a sutra at my father's bedside. Then we loaded him into a car, laying him down on a futon, and took him to the Department of Pathology

---

14. Danaid eggflies (メスアカムラサキ in Japanese) are a species of four-footed butterfly. Its scientific name is *hypolimnas misippus*.

15. Jean-Henri Fabre (1823–1915) was a French entomologist famous for his study of insects.

at Tokyo University for an autopsy, which was performed by Professors Miyake Masashi and Hirafuku Ichirō.

With some difficulty we removed the kimono from his rigid body and shifted him to the autopsy table. The autopsy room was nearly empty; its floor was bare concrete, and it was quite cold. My father's naked body was surprisingly skinny. His arms and legs were little more than skin and bones, and his pelvis and rib cage stood out prominently. The abdominal area was beginning to change color and was tepid, the warmth coming from the decay inside, which provided an odd reminder of life.

With a scalpel a slit was made from my father's throat down to his pubic bone, all in one smooth motion. The abdominal skin and muscle were quickly removed and his intestines were exposed. Also the rib cage was opened and his chest cavity revealed. His left lung was stiffly attached and was not removed easily. I was watching the pathologists' expert movements, along with my brother and uncle, who was also a medical doctor. I felt I should be grateful to my father for his letters, because having specialized in medicine now let me observe his corpse being autopsied without flinching.

We could see a great deal of calcification at the apex of his lung. In his right lung, tumors had formed an egg-sized hardened lesion. The right ventricle of his heart was enlarged, and his arteries were so stiff that they could be described as "crunchy." His kidneys had contracted to half of their normal size, as the medulla had cut into them and the cortex was narrowed down to a thin line. His scalp was removed and his skull sawed open. His grayish-white brain, which looked as if it were covered by gelatin, had also shrunk, as if shriveled up. In short, just about every part of his body was used up and exhausted. As I thought, he was at the point where dying was inevitable. That fact filled me with relief and pity at the same time.

At around one twenty in the afternoon, the autopsy was finished. The blood on his legs and arms was wiped off, the incisions were sutured, and he was placed back on the stretcher. Shavings were put into his abdominal cavity, and after his head was sutured he looked pretty much as he did before the autopsy.

We brought him back home and placed him in a coffin. We slid him in onto a mattress and then removed the mattress, stuffed paper pillows around him, and closed the lid. The house was chaotic with visitors coming to pay their respects and express condolences. There had been a cold rain all day until evening.

The cremation was two days later. The chanting of the sutra started at nine in the morning, then the lid was taken off the coffin so we could view him one last time, and we put flowers around his face, which looked paler, thinner, sharper, colder, and more sunken than the day before yesterday. His eyes were firmly closed. Surrounded by colorful flowers, his pale face looked even smaller. The ridge of his nose looked pointed. In the end, the youngest, infant daughter of my older brother was brought over in someone's arms. When the baby looked inside the coffin, she cheerfully, excitedly, and happily uttered, "Grandpa." My younger sister cried even harder. My older sister, who herself had been hysterical for a long while, scolded the younger sister for weeping, but the older sister's face was the most unsightly from her own tears. She told me angrily to give her my handkerchief as she had left hers downstairs.

The coffin left the house a little after ten. When we arrived at the crematorium, the sky was filled with soft, spring light. My younger sister could not stop crying, and my older sister, who looked angry, could not stop scolding her.

After a long wait, we gathered my father's bones and ashes. It was quick and businesslike. We put the remains into two urns, so we could bury one in his hometown of Yamagata. There were still some embers glowing red among his bones in the metal containers. The bones looked very white and frothy. "Father, you've finally turned to bones," I thought. After returning home, once again there was a sutra chanting.

My diary entry:

> The time passes while doing this and that, the house is in a great hubbub, and I just feel so tired. Yesterday it was especially crowded. We gave numbered tickets at the foyer for their overcoats and shoes, but it was chaotic with people coming and going. At night, it finally grew quiet. We've put all the flowers delivered to the house into the

> room where the altar is. The room is filled with flowers and looks beautiful.

The entry for the following day:

> At around ten at night, most of the guests had returned home. My mother told me to go to bed, but then she opened the door and came into the room. At around eleven, Keiko (my older brother's daughter) woke up and was too excited to get back to sleep. Moichi (my older brother's son) also did not sleep easily. It may be that the stress of the adults has been transmitted to the children.
>
> At around eleven thirty, I could finally take a bath. I'm exhausted.

The diary entry two days later:

> The funeral. Warm rain fell all night long but thankfully it stopped by morning. Sky overcast, but relatively warm. It was just so gloomy. Sutra chanting started at nine thirty in the morning. It started to drizzle again right before our departure to the temple where the funeral was held. I held the mortuary tablet.
>
> In the evening, we saw Uncle Shirobei and others off, then went to the Lion in Ginza with some people associated with the Araragi School and drank a fair amount of beer. Mr. Satō Satarō told me this story: when I was little, I pointed out either my father's scissors or knife and asked him, "Papa, if you die, will you give this to me?" My father later told Mr. Satō, "Children are strange, already thinking about their parents' death."
>
> Came home at eight. First night in many days that no visitor came. Only the gas heater was making sounds in the quiet room. Our mother brought our father's filthy pajamas and towels, and distributed them to my brother and me. She needed to clean up things quickly, she said, because she would not live long, either. I was told that, at ten at night, Ms. K. K. (a mental patient who had been asking my father to marry her for a long time) knocked at our already closed door, burned incense as people normally do, and left.

I remained in Tokyo for eight more days. One night, I opened my father's urn, took out four or five pieces of bone, and wrapped them in paper. I went back to Sendai with them. I wrote in my diary, "I drank beer in the dining car. The price of beer is down to 145 yen."

After returning to my boarding house I tried hard to study for the medical exam, but it did not go as smoothly as I had hoped.

My diary entry: "I drank urgently, bar hopping at Suntory Bar, Number One, Nagisa, etc."

I went on dreaming as frequently and vividly as always. I often dreamed about the landscape of Aoyama, where my house used to stand, and unlike before, I also had sentimental dreams about my father quite frequently.

And I still had some silly dreams about sex.

> The dream I had at dawn. S was there. It seemed I caressed her cheek a little. Then I realized that she was lying down and naked from the waist up. Her breasts were, to my puzzlement, sagging, yet they cast a dark shadow and were beautiful. It was as if I were looking at a famous painting. The dream was black and white, yet her naked body had dark shadows as if it were in an oil painting. After staring at her for a while, I said something about how beautiful she looked. And she quickly lifted her head, looked very shy, and tried to hide her breasts ...

himalayan hyōtantsugi

Himaraya no Hyōtantsugi

ヒマラヤのヒョウタンツギ

In the Himalayas is a region called Karakoram, which means "black gravel" in the Kyrgyz language. There are peaks that are over twenty-two thousand feet high.

I went there as the team doctor for a mountaineering expedition.

The villages at the foot of the mountains were extremely poor, and there was no doctor in the region, so a lot of people from the sur-

---

Hyōtantsugi. © Tezuka Productions. Reproduced with permission.

rounding villages came to me to get medications for their ailments. Some were suffering from dysentery, and some had tumors that attracted swarms of flies. Some had eye diseases, and it was very difficult for me to apply their eye medication, because they would open their mouths wide and close their eyelids.

But they were very happy to receive these medicines, and in appreciation they gave us tiny potatoes and cherries—tokens of their utmost thanks.

Children would often gather around with curiosity and watch us. Whenever I threw out empty medicine boxes, they would run to pick them up with big smiles on their faces.

One day a young boy came to us from a faraway village. There were scratches all over his feet, as he had walked a long way and had no shoes. I was told that his father was seriously ill and the boy needed medicine to take back to him. When I gave him the medicine, he said something with a humiliated expression on his face. According to our translator, the boy said, "My family is very poor, so I have nothing to give you in return. But I will surely repay you in the near future."

"Don't worry about it," I said and let him go home. Other members of our team gave him caramels and chewing gum. He trudged back toward home, carefully carrying all the things we had given to him.

That night, after the prayers to Allah and the chanting by our hired porters had ended, the camp grew quiet and I slept.

Then suddenly I was being shaken awake. It was the young boy. He offered me something. I was surprised, because it was something I knew only from comic books: *Hyōtantsugi*.[1]

"Where did you get this?" I asked him. He spoke and made a gesture of climbing a mountain.

"Oh, I see. This grows like mushrooms on top of the rocky mountains. Is that what you are saying?"

He looked as if he were ashamed to give me such a gift.

"Don't be embarrassed," I urged him. "You know, this is extremely

---

1. Hyōtantsugi is a famous comic character from Tezuka Osamu's cartoons. It is said to be a mushroom with a piglike face.

rare. This is not something we could ever buy with money. If I bring this back to Japan, I can only imagine how many kids will be delighted to see it."

The boy smiled happily as if he understood my words. I fell back to sleep, holding Hyōtantsugi very tightly.

When I awoke the next morning, I realized this must have all been a dream: the Hyōtantsugi was gone.

But I was too busy all day to feel disappointed, because we were all preparing for our departure. When our expedition members and porters were ready to leave, I caught sight of the boy among the villagers seeing us off and waving their hands. For the longest time he just kept waving his hand at us.

●●●

the captain

Senchō

船長

Until very recently, I was wandering, like Alice in Wonderland, in a mysterious world that had cast a kind of spell on me.

The city of Alexandria looked orderly on the surface, but in its back alleys everything was chaos and filth. Walls of buildings were falling down, streets were choked with dust, and the smell of horse manure hung in the air. Over here people were shouting to hawk their fruits and vegetables from pushcarts, over there people were greasing hot iron griddles to bake flatbread.

In contrast to these noisy vendors was an old man with gray hair quietly sitting on a chair in a house with sloping eaves. And a man dressed in long, white clothes, squatting down perfectly still. And people sipping coffee silently while playing a game that looked like *shōgi*.[1]

The scene suggested sluggishness and corruption and was the epitome of poverty and the mundane. Walking through those back alleys, I was drawn into a world that was both spiritless and brilliant. But I always returned to my senses, in a sad awakening, because I

1. *Shōgi* is often called Japanese chess.

would come out onto a broad main street where a train ran. Under a fierce sun that bleached the pale blue sky, the bustling cars and rushing train always shattered my enchantment.

I was serving as ship's doctor on a Fishery Agency tuna survey ship. Two days before at the port of Alexandria we offloaded a crew member who had been suffering from chronic appendicitis. He was to have surgery there, as that is outside my specialization and I did not have the confidence to operate on him myself.

The captain and other officers left to visit Cairo, but because of my responsibility as the ship's doctor, I stayed on board and then visited my patient in the hospital. When off duty, I wandered around the town and fell under its mysterious spell.

The hospital was on the main street. One evening, I was walking back to the port when a large figure suddenly blocked my way. I am not short, but this fellow loomed like a giant in my strangely tranquilized mind.

His hair was graying, his nose was sharp, and his dark brown skin was coarse. In contrast, his brown eyes were sparkling with softness.

He asked me in English, "Are you Japanese?"

"Yes," I replied.

"Are you a crew member of the Shōyō-maru?"

"Yes, I'm the ship's doctor."

"Is that so? I've read about the Shōyō-maru in the newspaper." He spoke boldly, extending his hand, so I immediately extended mine and we shook hands. The skin of his palm was hard and his grip was strong.

The Shōyō-maru was about to set out for long-line fishing in the Red Sea with local ichthyologists[2] on board. This joint Japanese-Egyptian expedition was probably the reason for the newspaper article.

Proudly he told me, "I'm a captain. I was a captain for a long time."

I looked at him again. He was wearing an old brown suit but had a new red tie fitted loosely around his neck. He was burly and about

---

2. An ichthyologist is a marine scientist who studies fish species.

six inches taller than I. His age was probably close to seventy, though I hadn't noticed that earlier.

I murmured stupidly, "Really …"

He went on, "I can sail the boat without having xxx. For forty years I was sailing to ______ and ______ in the Red Sea."

The xxx was probably some kind of navigation gear I was not familiar with, and ________ was the name of a place, but I did not understand that, either.

"Stars, you know, as long as I can see stars, I can sail any ocean," bragged the old man in a childlike way.

"Mikasa. Do you know the Mikasa, Doctor?" he asked.

He must have been talking about the warship Mikasa. I nodded.

He looked upward as if he were recalling something pleasant.

"I have a model of the Mikasa in my house. Japanese captains used to visit me in my house."

I suspected he had retired a long time ago and now had no visitors.

"I'm going out for dinner with my friend," he said, checking his watch, "but why don't you come over to my house later tonight? You can bring other crew members as well. Is the captain here too?"

"He's in Cairo now."

"Too bad. Well, let me give you my address."

He took a notebook out of his inside pocket and began writing. His fingers trembled a little. He licked his pencil once. His lips were thick.

He tore the page off and gave it to me. "If you show this to a cab driver, he'll know where it is. I can't offer you a meal because I'm going out to see someone now, but I'll be home by seven-thirty."

He extended his hand.

"By all means, please come. See you then."

"I'll try," I answered, not knowing what else to say.

When I returned to the ship and went up the ladder, I bumped into the chief officer, whom I called "Chofficer" for fun.

"Chofficer, I met a man who called himself a captain," I told him, describing the old man. "Would you like to go to his house with me tonight? He seemed like an interesting person, but I don't know how long it would take to get there."

"Let's ask this guy," said the officer and showed the paper to an Egyptian watchman on deck. They exchanged some words.

"No way, Doctor. He says the address is very far away, about forty minutes by car."

"Forty minutes …"

Back then the availability of foreign currencies was quite restricted, so none of us had much money.

"Instead, why don't we go to the place we went to last night?" he asked. "That would be much more fun."

"All right. Let's do that, then."

We could buy several glasses of liquor for what a forty-minute taxi ride would cost. I felt slightly guilty about the old captain and his model Mikasa, but I was easily swayed by the chief officer's suggestion.

And so, after supper, we went to the Hollywood bar. But we were rather disappointed. I was sort of hoping that a pretty girl would show up, but the only ones who came to our table were two old women who had also been with us the night before. They were very kindhearted: we had been led to that bar the previous night by a con man, and the women told us that he was a swindler who contracted with the bar and took a commission, so they warned us not to deal with him anymore.

Two days later, the Shōyō-maru left Alexandria for the Red Sea. The eldest of the ichthyologists was Professor G, who seemed close to seventy years old and was short and heavy. He had rheumatism and brought his own injectable medication, which he asked me to administer. Every morning after breakfast, I went to Professor G's cabin with a sterilized syringe and injected the medication into his arm. The instructions called for intramuscular injection, so I thought it would be safer and less painful to inject it in his hip, but I felt that I was not in a position to suggest it. The professor bared his arm and nodded at it, and after the shot, he always said in a husky voice, "Thank you, Doctor."

"You're welcome," I would say, and that was about all the conversation I had with him. Whenever I looked at the plump professor, I could not help thinking of the old captain who was so tall and whose eyes were so soft. When I had invited Chofficer to the captain's house, had I not fantasized that a very pretty granddaughter might greet us? I confess that I had. When you spend a long time out at sea, you think things you'd never think on land.

As time passed, though, I began to imagine that the captain was actually very lonely, and his wife may have died long ago, and he probably had no children or they lived far away. He was not dressed poorly when I met him, but he probably is not affluent either, and the furniture in his house must be old. He must have many model ships covered in dust, one of which is the Mikasa. In a house where people seldom come to visit, he quietly remembers his past, back when he had an active career. I also imagined that when he told me he couldn't offer us a meal, it was because he had nobody there to cook for guests. If we had visited his dark, dusty rooms that evening, he would have repeated his bragging under the influence of a little alcohol: "I don't need xxx. As long as I can see the stars, I can sail anywhere."

As the days crept slowly by, I kept pondering this. Late one night when the ship was heading through the Suez Canal, I was lying down on the upper bridge, my eyes fixed on the flat, deep-black desert on both sides. The temperature had dropped sharply at night in the desert. I put on a jacket but still felt chilly.

"Once I pass through this canal," I thought, "Japan will be much closer." Memories of Japan and my childhood, this voyage that we have been on for four months, the back alleys of Alexandria that held me spellbound all came to mind with an odd sentimentality. "Thank you, Doctor" in Professor G's husky voice, "I'm a captain" in the old man's strained but bold voice—then a pang of regret that I did not go to visit the old captain that night. No matter how much I regretted it, there was absolutely nothing I could do about it now.

In the meantime, as I shivered in harmony with the rhythm of the ship's engine, we floated slowly onward in the calm channel flanked by dark desert.

"As long as I can see the stars …"
Those big, bright, shining stars were piercing my eyes.

at the mouth of the river

Kakō nite

河口にて

♎♎♎

I heard a bell, so faint and far away it could have been an auditory hallucination. Or the sound might have been there continuously. While wondering about it, I was hurriedly lining up gleaming silver scalpels and forceps. I turned toward the operating table, but it was an old-fashioned, age-darkened wooden bed. On it lay a flaxen-haired girl wrapped in a blanket. Her slender face had the complexion of wax, and as soon as she closed her wide eyes, I could no longer recall what color they were. I reached out my hand and pulled the blanket off, exposing her white abdomen, where a surgical field was marked out in gauze. The razor-sharp scalpel barely touched her thin skin and cut it smoothly, like slicing soft raw fish. Soon it touched a thick blood vessel and her blood gushed like a toy fountain. I wondered why it was not red. Even when I compressed the vessel with forceps, the steady bleeding didn't stop. Yet I kept moving my hand, slowly cutting open the muscle layer and finally reaching the whitish peritoneum. I stroked it lightly with the tip of the scalpel and a dark abdominal cavity appeared. There were no snaky intestines in it. I put my hand in and fumbled around. My fingers touched a warm fleshy mass in the back. I pulled out the slimy thing and realized that it was a compactly curled fetus. It had dark red blood clots here and there, but it had a full face with eyes and nose. It was twitching at first but stopped moving in my hand before long, and I could feel its lukewarm body growing cold. I peered down at the girl's waxy face while holding the dead fleshy mass. She too seemed to have stopped breathing and her eyes remained closed. At this point, for the first time, I felt shocked.

"Doctor."

The voice echoed in the dark. As I awoke, I found myself lying on a narrow bed in a ship's cabin. I hurriedly opened the curtain and saw a pale face, just like the one in the dream, but this one was bearded. He hesitantly called me one more time.

"Doctor?"

I forced myself to move my limbs, though they didn't feel like my own. I climbed down from the bunk bed. Inside the cabin was strangely dark and I could only see a dim, whitish light through a circular window.

The man, standing in the dim light, didn't look real. "Doctor, I feel like I'm going to throw up," he said in a gasping voice. I must have fallen asleep without leaving my desk light on. In the pale light from the porthole window, I could barely see his face. I finally turned on the light and recognized a young crewmember from the engine room. He was pressing on his chest with one hand, and his stubble-covered face was wan and clammy with cold sweat. I shook my head and tried to wipe away my sleep.

It had been three months since this small, six-hundred-ton tuna survey ship left Japan. The drinking water we loaded at a European port was bad and several of the crew were complaining of nausea. As ship's doctor, I prepared medicine ahead of time so I could give it to patients as soon as it was needed; however, this guy's nausea was clearly more severe, so an oral medication wasn't going to work. He even had a difficult time talking. I laid him down on a sofa, went into the treatment room next to my chamber, and browsed through boxes of injection drugs. My brain was still clouded and I couldn't make up my mind what drug I should use, but I finally chose an ampule and administered the injection awkwardly into his arm. He was in a cold sweat and the shot didn't seem to be good enough to make him feel better, so with my foggy brain, I tried to come up with what to do next. However, as I was still rubbing his arm, a voice that sounded like some different person said, "Doctor, I feel much better," and he wiped the sweat from his forehead. There was no way the drug could work so quickly, so I suggested that he lie down a little longer, but he insisted he was fine, bowed clumsily, and quickly left the cabin.

I finally, really woke up after he had gone, and I felt very cold as I was moving around only in my sleepwear. I peeked into the lower bunk, but the third officer with whom I shared the cabin wasn't there. He might be on duty on the bridge. Shivering in my sleepwear though the heat was on, I plugged in a space heater. The clock on the wall indicated six o'clock, so the dawn hadn't completely arrived. The foggy view through the porthole revealed that the ship hadn't moved all night. I huddled in front of the space heater where nichrome wires finally glowed red.

Wearing sleepwear on a ship may sound strange. However, because this was a Japanese Fishery Agency vessel, we didn't care what we looked like. So I wore my sleepwear every night. After more than three months without washing, it was grimy and dirty. I kept thinking that I'd wash it on the next laundry day, but when that day came I always forgot, almost as if on purpose.

Even huddling over the heater, I was cold all the way from my back to my feet in the unkempt sleepwear, but I felt this was the best thing I could do. I tried to think about things in the back of my head—the crewman who was nauseated, the girl in the dream whose baby I removed—everything was so hazy. In addition, in a very short period of time, I was recalling all sorts of things that had happened to me over the years, even the most trivial, mundane events. I had heard that if you fall off a cliff, many past events race through your mind in a fraction of a second. There might be some truth to that. I was giving serious thought to these odd things.

Still cold, I slowly put on a shirt and underwear that I had crumpled up and thrown next to my stool. Though still sleepy, I didn't feel like going back to bed; in fact, I felt an urge somewhere in my heart, so I finished dressing and left the cabin, without any apparent purpose.

As I came up onto the rear deck, I saw the ship was surrounded by fog. Everywhere I looked was just whiteness, with no horizon line between sky and sea. To be precise, we weren't out to sea yet, just at the mouth of a river. Two days had passed since we left the Port of Antwerp but we still hadn't entered the ocean.

All we could do was drop anchor where the sea water and the river mixed together and wait. We floated in place on the placid water that reflected the blank, white fog. Up on the bridge I could see a blue lamp that was used for communicating with river pilots. Such a dim light could never reach the land, and I had no clue where the land was anyway. It was quiet, the fog moving along soundlessly; fine drops of water drifted like smoke in front of me standing on the deck.

The dawn must have broken—the whitish light mixed with the mist revealed the outlines of our small ship. A foghorn sounded from far away, and then, unexpectedly close by, another erupted like an ancient mythological giant groaning. In fact, there was no better word than "erupt" to describe the way the foghorn blasted. The eruption of that foghorn blast disappeared into the many layers of dense fog, and the next thing I heard was someone striking a bell. Evidently a ship was sailing in this dense fog, and suddenly foghorns and bells were sounding everywhere, signaling each other to indicate their locations. The sounds echoed heavily, as if from the far corners of the earth, and because the bells were so faint, they seemed even more melancholy. Afterward what was left was fog and a hushed silence. Suddenly my own ship blared its foghorn. I was so close to the foghorn that I jumped out of my skin—it nearly blew out my eardrums. I smiled wryly. Then I saw the shadow of a person moving on the bridge: a duty seaman, awkward in a thick overcoat, repeatedly banging a bell. This also echoed loudly, but once it stopped, the scary, absolute quiet returned.

Without my coat, I started to feel cold. Almost sleepwalking, I went down the gangway and back to my cabin. We had no idea when the ship would sail, let alone arrive at our next port, in France. I had heard from a longtime friend that he was sick in bed in France. He had been my friend since high school and had been studying in France for about three years. His scholarship must have expired a long time ago, so I wondered how he was getting by. No doubt he was living in poverty. Both of us were bad correspondents, but we resumed writing letters after I went to sea. We had exchanged letters at each port I stopped in, and I was looking forward to visiting him more than anything else. It was at a port in Holland that I received not his usual, closely written letter in small handwriting, but a hastily sent postcard. He had fallen ill and apparently asked a girl he knew to mail the card for him.

The girl, born in Lisbon, was fourteen, lived with her mother in the neighborhood of his apartment, and for some reason or other often went to visit him. Other than the girl, he didn't seem to get any visitors. The girl kept several small animals in her apartment, and she told him cute little stories—like when she put her mouse on the table and it sipped wine from a glass, or when she accidentally dropped her little turtle from her third-floor window and healed the crack in its shell by putting scotch tape on it. Except for recounting her stories, his letters to me were usually gloomy, dark, and wet, like Europe in winter. I could clearly sense the depressing Parisian winter and the darkness of his poorly lit apartment. I could even imagine the things he didn't write about. In my mind's eye, his room was on the fourth floor of an old building, at the top end of a long, dark, and worn wooden winding staircase. He seldom went out but sat at a small desk, spending his time turning the pages of a book with a worn cover, going to the kitchen to boil water, or breaking a baguette of white bread and chewing it as he sat on his bed. At the moment, I felt he was too ill to get up and was just laying on his squeaky bed, with his skinny face, and with the girl from Lisbon sitting on the edge of the bed, utterly powerless, not knowing what to say. He didn't have money for a doctor, which is why I needed to go to see him and give him some medication as soon as possible.

Under normal conditions, it takes less than a day to sail from Antwerp in Belgium to Le Havre in France. But we lost four days in Antwerp, and when we were finally able to depart, we were beset by fog again. Two days after departing Antwerp, we were still at the mouth of the river, waiting.

While waiting in Antwerp, I had grown more concerned for my friend; I feared that his sickness was more serious than just an ordinary cold. The fog lasted for several more days. The local people were saying that this was the first time in thirty years they had seen so much fog lasted so long. At the mouth of the river, dozens of ships were stopped, some were coming in and some going out, and none had any idea when they could sail from port. We were not allowed to go ashore during the day because of our ship's stand-by status, but when it was decided in the evening that our departure would again be postponed, we were permitted to disembark. I had spent all of my Belgian currency, so there was nothing much I could do to have fun in town; mostly I walked around aimlessly with the collar of my overcoat turned up. Yellowish car headlights and lines of streetlights were all blurred by the fog. On a busy street near the train station, I took out a U.S. dollar bill that I had set aside so I could use when necessary, purchased one or two postcards, and received my change in Belgian francs. Then after wasting time looking at movie posters and window-shopping outside a bookstore, I looked for an empty café where I could linger with a glass of beer. I repeated this every night. I thought of my sick friend: if we hadn't encountered this fog, I would be in his room by now. Might he be in love with the girl from Lisbon? No, she was only fourteen. But girls who grow up on European cheese mature quicker, so a fourteen-year-old could be like a grown woman. Et cetera, et cetera.

I counted my money and ordered one more glass of beer, but by the time I drank half of it, I felt quite drunk and wondered why on earth I was sitting alone in this place at this time. I attempted to recall some of the ports I had visited or places I had traveled by train, but all my memories became entangled. The same happened with the paintings and sculptures I had seen. Everything was a blur, as if wrapped in fog. In the café there were some families relaxing and groups of people laughing and drinking, and in one corner was an elderly woman with a birdlike face just sitting motionless for a long time, not touching the cup of tea in front of her. I imagined that she probably preferred being in a café with people's conversation, laughter, and music, rather than going back to her empty room and spending a hopeless night there. She embodied loneliness, sitting still there in her black overcoat. When I came to my senses, however, I realized that I too had been sitting at a table alone for a long time. I hurriedly called the waiter and paid my bill, leaving behind a little tip that I'd managed to calculate in the back of my mind. When I glanced at the old woman as I was leaving, she was still in the same position, looking down. It looked as if she were resigned to a destiny of sitting there into the night until all the cheerful people left the café. On the way back to port, it grew colder and foggier. Streetlights and headlights were blurry, and occasionally a shadowy person emerged from and then disappeared into the fog.

There was no use immersing myself in depressing memories, so I left my cabin again and went up to the bridge, this time through a narrow passageway below decks. Because the ship couldn't move, the officer on duty was writing something in the chart room, and a seaman in a thick overcoat was walking around the wheelhouse as if he had nothing to do. He sometimes went outside and rang the ship's bell, and in response bells rang from all around in the fog.

With a sullen face, the seaman murmured, "That's a frying pan, Doctor."

"A what?"

"That strange sound we just heard. They are banging on a frying pan."

"I hate that sound," said another seaman, frowning. "But that's an oil drum."

"No, it's a frying pan. An oil drum doesn't make that sound. I know it well."

Even such a conversation was not at all amusing. On the contrary, this conversation was a symptom of how frustrated and irritated everyone was. I didn't feel like making the effort to join the debate, so I asked if I could look at the radar. It showed that we were located a little short of the mouth of the river. The land was indicated by irregular yellow stripes, and in the estuary where the river flows into the ocean dozens of small yellow dots were shining, crowding the radar screen. Each dot was a ship forbidden to sail, anchored in the fog, and announcing its presence with bells and horns. Looking at the glowing cluster on the radar made me realize that there was no way we could leave and my concerns were renewed.

"It seems to be clearing off a little," said one of the seamen on watch.

On the starboard side, the haze did seem a little thinner. When I took a good look, I could make out the shape of a ship very near to us. Until that moment, it was an empty white world, but now a gigantic tanker of at least ten thousand tons was only a hundred yards away from us. It felt like an optical illusion. I went to the side of the bridge to get a better look at the giant iron hulk that was gradually appearing clearly. I felt a tiny thrill of satisfaction at discerning a clear image from what had previously been totally white. After a short while, I saw the silhouette of a person moving at the stern of the tanker and then heard the clear sound of a bell emanating from there. Quite suddenly, the silhouette faded—the fog was becoming dense again and, like magic, it swallowed the entire tanker just as it had emerged. It was incredible: no matter how much I strained my eyes trying to find the tanker, I could no longer see anything but fine particles of mist floating in the air.

I must have been wandering aimlessly below deck. I remembered warm air near the entrance of the engine room, and I recalled my skin, wet from the humidity that stealthily rolled into the passageway. But then I was on the foredeck, leaning forward from the side to look out on the surface of the undulating whitish water. Somewhere in my heart, I was still thinking about my friend confined in bed in his bleak room with the stained ceiling, and about the girl born in Lisbon helplessly looking at her middle-aged friend from a foreign land as if she were scrutinizing her turtle with its broken shell. Perhaps my concerns were groundless. My friend might have already recovered from his illness and the girl might have nothing more to worry about than letting her mouse drink wine. I knew this fog was wearing down everyone's spirits and engendering negative thoughts, but I couldn't help but worry about him.

The deck was wet all over even though it hadn't been hit by the waves, and the riggings were all wrapped by the mist. The lines and clasps had frozen in the cold weather near Germany and Holland, but now the weather was somewhat warmer and they were simply damp, which was annoying. Freezing is something closer to our perception, but fog irritates our peripheral senses, muffling them and returning them to a primitive or newborn state. I can only remember my infancy as a concept now, but I vaguely recollect the constant experience of irritating anxiety mixed with unclear expectations—just like now.

Suddenly I became aware of a black shadow in the middle of the blanket of white fog. It was a ship and, to my alarm, it was quietly coming right toward us. The ship had a shallow draft and I could see where the red anticorrosive paint was. In other areas the paint was worn off, as if the vessel had been drifting in the ocean for years. As it loomed closer, it was bigger than I had thought. I had to look upward at the bow, and there I saw a tall black man leaning on the rail and looking down at us. The ship was approaching quickly and quietly. It was now within my reach if I stretched out my arm, and I could clearly see the black man's facial features. Although I was convinced the ship would crash into us, I simply stood still with fear and anticipation, gazing at it and the man in its bow. He was both sneering and furrowing his brow with concern. His thick lips were tightly closed, and he kept leaning on the rail and looking down at us. The giant ship hovered over us, and at the moment it collided with us, it disappeared. In that instance, I found myself in bed in my cabin. I couldn't tell what had really happened and what had been a dream, and I didn't have the energy to think about it.

I had my clothes on, so I guess I had been up and dressed at one time. Or who knows—I could have slept with my clothes on the previous night. I got out of bed and looked at the dense whiteness outside the porthole. I shook my head and left my cabin, this time with my overcoat on. I half-ran to the front deck, very aware of my own heartbeat, and looked down at the undulating water surface, which reflected nothing but fog. The fog melting into the water and the water melting into the fog were writhing with the waves. Usually when a ship stops its engine at sea, you can hear the water slapping the ship's side but I heard nothing, as if the water were dead. A little ahead, it was difficult to distinguish the sky from the water, but the sky looked just barely brighter. A barrel was bobbing on the whitish surface, but the tide was pulling it and it melted into the fog fairly quickly.

Out of nowhere I heard the faint sound of an engine. I thought it was just my imagination, but the next moment I could hear that it was a motorboat. I ran up the ladder and looked toward the sound but couldn't see anything. In such a lifeless world where we heard only foghorns and the sound of bells, the familiar hot-bulb engine sounded wonderfully nostalgic. I peered impatiently, and eventually it made its appearance on our opposite side. It felt unreal. I could identify two or three figures on a white midsized boat. Thinking it might be a river pilot, I climbed down the ladder and approached it.

A small fellow in a black leather jacket stood on tiptoe at the bow and spoke to a cabin boy on the deck. The cabin boy didn't seem to understand him and looked at me with a puzzled expression on his face.

"Are you a pilot?" I uttered. My voice sounded like a stranger's voice that I was hearing for the very first time.

The small man shook his head and said something very quickly that I didn't understand. Then he said in laborious, heavily accented English, "Is this a Danish ship?"

"No, this is a Japanese ship. Aren't you a pilot?" I asked again.

He shook his head as if to say no. "Have you seen a Danish ship?"

"Danish?" I repeated.

Here the second officer who was on duty came and took over for me. In the stern of the boat stood two women, shivering in their overcoats. One was elegant-looking, elderly, with a somewhat rugged face, and the other, probably her daughter, was blond and around twenty years old. Both were quiet but showed evident exhaustion. There were suitcases at their feet. The small man in the bow was obsessively repeating, "Danish ship?"

"We don't know. There are three ships over on this side," said the second officer and pointed to the right into the impenetrable fog. "Have you tried there?"

"They were not Danish."

The man looked displeased, while the two women stayed motionless, looking down at the water as if indifferent to the conversation.

"On this side, too," the second officer said, gesturing in the opposite direction, "there seem to be more ships. Anyway, we haven't seen a Danish one."

"Okay," the small man said at last and shrugged his shoulders—his air of defeat made quite an impression on me. He cued his partner who was steering the boat and the sad sound of its little motor echoed once again. As the white boat was departing, the man raised his fingers to his forehead in a salute and said, "Good luck." The two women looked very sad, the elegant elderly one staring down motionlessly at the water and the young one looked at us briefly, her blond hair making her expression even gloomier. Standing in a trance, I listened to the engine putt-putting away into silence as the boat and its figures were swallowed up in the whiteness.

"They were women, right?"

"Yeah."

I heard the whispers behind me. Watchkeepers on the deck had come down to see the boat and were engaged in meaningless on and off conversation, in the same way they were discussing the sound of the pan or drum.

"Hair ..."

"What?"

"The hair, the color of her hair. When I look at hair that color, I feel sad."

"Sad, you said?"

"Yeah, sad about floating in this strange foreign sea."

"Don't be silly," another voice said. "By the way, wasn't her belly big?"

"What do you mean?"

"It was big. It was obvious even with her overcoat. Right, Doctor?"

Suddenly being addressed, I looked back to see who was speaking. It was a member of the engine-room crew who had come to see me in a cold sweat. He looked perfectly fine, not like someone who had been very sick that morning.

"That young woman was pregnant. Don't you think so, Doctor?"

"Um, I didn't notice."

But I began to think he was right. Just then I noticed a taste bitter as a sleeping pill spreading in my mouth. The boat was now long gone across the white, wavering water but I could still hear its distant engine. I shook my head irritatedly and asked him, "Didn't you come to see me this morning?"

I knew it was a strange question. He looked confused for a moment but responded quickly, "I'm fine now. I'm totally okay."

So at least it wasn't an illusion that he had come to see me, I thought absentmindedly.

"This is really boring, isn't it, Doctor?" he said briskly. His upbeat voice contrasted with how everyone else was feeling so it was even more annoying. "When on earth can we get out of here?"

I collected myself and, just to make conversation, replied, "What day is it today?" It was as if my voice had come out on its own from somewhere else in my body. But he took my question seriously, inclined his head and mumbled, "Let me see, today is, uh … the twelfth? No, I don't know. It has been so foggy every day. Just give me a moment …"

"It's the twelfth," a watchkeeper next to him interrupted.

"You're right, it's the twelfth," nodding his head, he looked almost happy. "The twelfth it is! So, it's eight in the morning on February the twelfth now."

I nodded. But knowing the date didn't change anything. On the contrary, it disheartened me. I left the crewmembers and strolled aimlessly around the wet deck, then looked out from the other side. Layers of cold, whitish water were undulating, and everything was indistinct, melting together. Even the very essence of who I am seemed to be blurred and absorbed into the water. The dense fog didn't seem to clear off at all. Somewhere from far off, again like an auditory hallucination, I heard the sound of bells that didn't seem to belong to this world.

≏≏≏

yellow ship

Kiiroi fune

黄いろい船

❍❍❍

"Chie."

A man was calling his child's name. Lying on his back in a six-mat room in his apartment, he absentmindedly called to his four-year-old daughter, who was playing house behind him.

"What, Daddy?"

She was a quiet, well-behaved girl. When she came home from preschool, she usually played alone, but she also enjoyed helping her mother. The man's wife was a little concerned that the girl was too reserved and shy with strangers.

"Okay, I will feed you." She was talking to a small doll. She spoke very clearly only when talking to a doll.

"Chie."

"What? Okay, Mister Chestnut, open your mouth."

"Mister Chestnut again?"

"Yes, this is Mister Chestnut."

The girl had fallen in love with chestnuts when she saw a picture of them with their spiny burs, in a picture book. Last year when the man took her out of town and she saw real chestnuts on a tree, she was even more delighted. The man occasionally bought roasted sweet chestnuts for her, but she lined them up and played with them rather than eat them. At night, she went to bed with the chestnuts lined up near her pillow.

The shabby doll she was playing with now was named Mister Chestnut because it had a round face, although there were no other resemblances between the doll and a chestnut.

"Chie," said the man one more time. "Tell me the story of Mister Chestnut."

"Sure," she responded offhandedly. "Ghost and Mister Chestnut talked to each other …"

While lying there on a tatami mat, he listened to his daughter's monotone voice.

"Then, there appeared Mister Mouse."

The man was looking at the low ceiling and, hung on a dirty wall, a calendar that was too big for the small apartment room.

"Let's go to Miss Bride," the girl said very seriously. "Miss Bride, please come here. Yes, yes," she said "Yes, yes," in a feigned feminine voice.

The man glanced sideways at the calendar. It had a color photograph of a famous place for each month, but it was too flashy and it matched neither the room nor his psyche.

"There came Ghostly Tulip and—"

"Ghostly Tulip?" the man reflexively asked. "What's that, Chie?"

"It's a very beautiful tulip," she answered. "Then everyone went into a castle. In the castle, there were …"

"That old word 'castle,'" he thought. Every child loves a castle, and he used to as well.

"There was a pretty bride. Ghost, Mister Chestnut, and Mister Mouse …"

"The word 'bride' sounds good, too. The words that children use are all good," he thought.

"… then everyone had a feast. Okay, the end."

"Is that the end?"

"That's all. Right, Mister Chestnut?"

"That's all … huh," the man mumbled to himself. Then he drew his head back and looked at his own daughter. The girl, reflected on his eyes upside down, was still very young. She was looking down and doing something with the doll. Although she was his daughter, he didn't think she was good-looking, yet she looked as adorable as a doll. It seemed to make sense that she was befriended by the Ghostly Tulip, Mister Chestnut, and the castle.

He heard the door open. His wife set down a shopping bag filled with vegetables and paper bags in the narrow entryway, and the girl ran to her and began taking things out one by one.

"Chie, the leeks have dirt on them, so be careful."

"You bought a lot."

"Oh, there are eggs in there—please don't break them."

The man slowly stood up and walked over to them.

"You bought so much," he said, looking at his wife's face.

She had an ordinary egg-shaped face and that's what he liked about her. Of course, she no longer had the fresh look, like a newly laid egg, that she had when they first met.

"We'll have sukiyaki tonight," the wife said, lining up the eggs in the refrigerator.

"I've got really good meat. Look at this."

She opened the wrapper to show a stack of thin slices of meat, brutally red, marbled with white fat in a beautiful pattern. The meat slices were piled thick and nearly spilling out of the imitation bamboo-skin wrapper.

"Marbled beef," the man said brusquely. "Beef is expensive now, isn't it?"

"It's not cheap."

"Can we afford such a feast?"

"We should have a feast at a time like this."

The wife smiled, and put a big bundle of leeks on the narrow counter of the narrow kitchen.

"Thre-e-e, four-r-r," the girl was counting eggs in the rack on the refrigerator door.

"Fi-i-ive, si-i-ix. We need two more."

The rack had eight spaces and two were empty. The small empty spaces looked so big to him, although he had just seen the big stack of beautifully marbled meat.

"Chie, close the door or the ice will melt," the wife said.

"Uh-huh," the girl nodded and said as she closed the refrigerator. "Mommy, eggs look like chestnuts."

At night, the man lay down on the floor and watched TV in his pajamas. The room was still very humid.

His television was an old set, and sometimes the screen showed stripes rolling upward. Adjusting the antenna or controls did not help, and he had to wait patiently for the screen to come back to normal.

Because he'd eaten too much, his stomach felt depressingly heavy.

"No-good crap," he said and turned off the TV. "Not one decent program."

"Let's sleep," said the wife. She had been sitting on the floor, knitting.

"Eat and sleep," the man said apologetically. "I feel guilty."

"You will find a job again soon," she said, pushing her knitting things to the side of her pillow. "You are a hard worker by nature."

"That's why I am upset!" the man blurted in a sudden rage. "I was betrayed. Twelve years I worked—there was no need for them to fire me. There were a lot of lazy people but …"

"Better stop it now," the wife said gently. She was a very gentle person, almost as if she were born to calm other people. "Everything is luck. Soon good luck will come to you."

"I am not interested in working anymore," the man mumbled to himself. "I don't want to work."

"Then you should just hang around for a while," the wife said kindly. She was smiling, not showing the slightest worry.

"But what's going to happen to us if I don't work?" the man said in a defeated tone.

"I'll go to work again," she said.

"But we have a kid."

"You will take care of her, won't you?"

He fell silent and lit a cigarette.

"Really, you need to take it easy for a while." She wasn't comforting him but said this quite naturally. "You are tired, I know."

He looked at his wife. The familiar oval face was smiling surely, and she added, "Chie has been enjoying being able to take walks or play with her daddy."

"I don't think I have played with her that much," he thought. "At most, I made her tell me the story of Mister Chestnut."

"Yeah, I'll take a walk with her more often," he mumbled, stubbing out his cigarette in an ashtray. "I'll take her to and from preschool, too."

"That would be nice," the wife said, nodding.

"I just don't want to work. I don't like it anymore. I'm tired of it," the man said in one breath, like a child who can't let go of a topic.

"That's fine."

"I won't work until my unemployment insurance expires."

"That's a good idea. Even when the insurance expires, we'll be fine for a while."

The man looked at his wife and said as if he were sighing, "You never object."

"That's my nature. I can't help it."

"Having a good wife like you," he looked at the wall and said, "makes me even angrier."

"I'm sorry."

"Don't be a fool," he said softly. "You have no need to apologize to me."

Suddenly the girl, who had been sleeping in the corner of the room, said something. There was no space in the room after spreading three futon mattresses, and the girl's small mattress had been pushed into the corner. The voice from the corner sounded like she was talking in her sleep.

When he looked at her, her eyes were open and looking at him. She said in a small, contented voice, "Daddy."

"Yes?" he replied as if he were flustered. "Do you want to pee?"

She shook her head, abruptly smiled, looked at her side, and stroked the doll she had put near her pillow. Then, looking even more satisfied, she nestled her head on the pillow and closed her eyes. Soon, they could hear from her light breathing that she was asleep.

"She is happy because her daddy is always around," the wife said, straightening a blanket over her.

The man was silent for a while, then lay down on the futon mattress.

"I wonder if chestnuts are already on the trees."

"Eh?"

"Chestnuts, the real ones, in burs."

"They must be. It's almost autumn."

The wife prepared to go to sleep and yawned slightly.

"Let's take Chie to where chestnuts are growing. We'll take a train," he said, vacantly gazing up at the low ceiling.

"That would be nice. But don't you think there are chestnut trees around here?"

"I don't know. There may be, but I don't know where."

Still looking up at the ceiling, he continued, "There are houses everywhere around here. No wonder there are so many useless people."

The man went to his next appointment at the unemployment office.

He had gotten used to the stark building with its bare concrete walls, but he couldn't help feeling depressed among the people there, who all looked very tired, sitting on benches and waiting for their turns.

He stood up and went to look at posters on a wall. There was an ordinary poster to recruit trainees, and a notice warning, "You may encounter a person in and around the office who persistently talks to you. Please be careful not to be taken in." Another poster, which was new, read, "Overseas ventures: Now recruiting trainees as industrial technology immigrants." The South American continent was drawn in green, and the word "Brazil" stood out in bright white.

"South America," he thought. "I used to like these kinds of dreams."

The poster invited applicants between the ages of twenty-five and thirty-five, so he qualified by a narrow margin. But he had a degree in humanities and was not good with machines, so it was just a day-dream. Moreover, he had a wife and a daughter who were too good for him.

"If she were a nasty wife and Chie were an annoying kid, maybe then …"

He imagined himself being in that situation.

"Even so, I have no marketable skills."

He went back to the bench and sat down next to a middle-aged man who was wearing very worn clothes. The man was staring at the concrete floor, but sometimes he looked up and yawned. Meanwhile, a young woman in flashy clothes that didn't match the office's atmosphere promenaded past them.

His turn came. He walked behind a partition and up to an interview space that was a step higher than the floor. He went to one of the desks and sat down in front of an interviewer with whom he had long ago become familiar. He had the impression that this interviewer was a kind man. He had offered detailed advice and helped him in finding many different jobs. Today, though, his attitude was different, as if he were a different person. He was gruff and talked to the man as if he were interrogating him.

"Did you really even go there?"

He became more and more scornful as the interview went on.

"You might have earned that much salary before, but don't expect to receive the same when you start a new job."

The man apologized hesitantly and explained that it wasn't the salary he didn't like but he wasn't sure whether his skills fit the job.

"Skills? If you've got such skills, why are you unemployed? Don't take searching for a job lightly."

"Why do I have to listen to his lecture? If I had become a civil servant like this guy, I wouldn't have lost my job in the first place," he vaguely thought.

At last he received the two-week allowance. But to add to his misery, as he got up to leave, the interviewer said, "Isn't it about time you finally got a job? Everyone ought to work, you know."

At the building's exit, the man wasted some time pushing the door that he was supposed to pull.

In front of the door was a low concrete-block wall, and on top of that was a corrugated plastic wall. The blue plastic wall must have been bright and modern-looking when new, but now it was blackened and dirty, broken near the edge, and shabby with holes in it.

"I will never work," he grumbled angrily. "Why am I obliged to work?"

A line of cars was driving on the one-way street in front of the building, and he couldn't cross easily.

Rather than going back to the train station as usual, he turned into a narrow alley. There was a cheap restaurant with a sign for a "Pork Cutlet Lunch," a coffee shop where there seemed to be no customers, and a short-stay hotel that was quite new but looked seedy. At the corner was a small realtor's office that also looked dreary but it had numerous ads and some were pasted on the wall across the street. Some said "Japanese Restaurant for Sale: 80 Million Yen," and "Pinball Parlor for Sale: 75 Million Yen."

Absentmindedly the man was guessing that a pinball parlor would be a good business. The last time and the time before last when he visited the unemployment office, he had stopped at a pinball parlor on the way home. He hadn't gone into one for many years before that, so he was interested to see a new pinball machine called Tulip. He was also interested to find that the prizes had become more tasteful and homey. The last time he played, he won a horseshoe-shaped can of ham, but of course he had spent enough money to buy three cans.

"I shouldn't play pinball today," the man thought.

He had been thinking that he needed a haircut, and since he saw a barbershop with some empty chairs, he went in. But it was understaffed, so he had to wait on a sofa. There were two customers, both of whom were gazing upward while having their beards shaved.

The man picked up one of the magazines piled on the table and flipped through the pages randomly, then picked up another to browse through it.

He began reading an article entitled "The Man Who Imports His Dream Airship." He had liked airships when he was a boy, and the word "airship" seemed closely related to the word "dream."

The report was about a man who was so fascinated with airships that he devoted himself to chartering a medium-sized one owned by a German company and bringing it to Japan.

The article had subheadings like "200 Million Yen to Bring One Ship" and "A Challenge to Modern Mechanics." The article said this person didn't have enough money but was working alone diligently toward his goal in an office called the Japan Airship Organizing Office, which he had established in one room of a trading firm.

"This is a nice dream. I wouldn't mind working on a project like that," he thought. He nodded as he looked at a photo in the magazine, published last month, showing the airship with the logo of a foreign department store on its side.

The man suddenly remembered that a zeppelin had come to Japan before he had been born. His now-deceased father had witnessed it and used to tell him about it again and again when he was growing up. Even before then, an airship had flown through the Japanese sky:

Narrowing her eyes,
a woman stares
at the sky
as the yellow ship
passes through it

Through a February sky,
as the yellow ship
sails around,
I kiss her lips
with deep feeling[1]

---

1. Both poems were composed by Saitō Mokichi. They are included in *Shakkō* 赤光 (Red lights, 1913), Mokichi's first collection of poems. The original poems read:

The man remembered these short poems composed by a renowned poet at the beginning of the twentieth century. He wondered what kind of an airship it was. Was it a small, old Japanese military ship?

"Yellow ship ..." he murmured in his mind.

He could practically see the rounded body of a yellow ship leisurely floating over a filthy, gloomy city as if it were boundlessly drifting about.

"Yellow ship, huh," he mumbled again.

Just then a barber called him: "Sorry for the wait. It's your turn."

"Oh, okay."

He put the magazine down and stood up from the sofa, whose springs squeaked.

"Daddy, I found chestnuts!" The girl ran to him excitedly.

"Eh?" the man lying down said in a dubious voice.

He still had not taken his daughter into the countryside where chestnuts grow. In fact he was so lazy lately that he'd stopped taking her to and from preschool.

"Are you listening? Chestnuts, real ones," the girl persisted.

"Were they on a tree?"

"Uh-huh, they were on a tree. There were some on the ground, too."

His wife came in after the girl. The man, with a guilty look, looked up at her familiar face and asked, "Chie told me she found chestnuts—is that true?"

"Yes. Good job, Chie."

---

maboshige ni	まぼしげに
sora ni miirishi	空に見入りし
onna ari	女あり
ōshoku no fune	黄色のふね
ama haseyukeba	天馳せゆけば

nigatsu zora	二月ぞら
kiiroki fune ga	黄いろき船が
tobitareba	飛びたれば
shimijimi to onna ni	しみじみと女に
kuchifuru kanaya	口觸るかなや

The wife was smiling. She always smiled so innocently that he should surely be thankful to her.

"It was good but no fun," the girl said.

"Why not?"

"Because all the burs were empty."

Then the wife added, "When you turn the corner of the Shimizu's house, it's there near the next street. Who would have expected to find a chestnut tree so nearby? It's in a hidden spot. A big chestnut tree is at the gate."

"And the nuts were on the ground?"

"Yes, there were about ten burs in front of the garage, but all of them were empty. The kids in the neighborhood must have picked them up."

"Even burs are good. Why didn't you bring them home?"

"I don't like the burs," the girl interrupted. "A bur stung my finger."

"It's because you were in a rush and touched it," the wife said smiling.

"Chie, you like chestnuts in the bur, right?"

"Not any more. I only like the nuts inside," she said, sadly examining her finger.

"Chie," the man finally got up and said. "When new burs fall next time, let's go to pick them up together."

"Sure, Daddy. Then let's go now."

"The new burs haven't fallen yet, and you've just seen old ones, right?"

"But the wind has blown since then, so there may be some new ones on the ground."

Her face had a distant look as if she were a grown-up.

"Not yet. The burs are still green. There will be plenty of them falling to the ground soon. Trust me, I'll find a lot of burs that have chestnuts in them."

"Okay," the girl replied with an energetic nod. "Then I can put real chestnuts and Mister Chestnut together in bed."

"Yeah, that's a good idea."

While saying this, the man pulled the girl gently into his arms and smelled her hair.

In the corner of a store window stood a cylindrical floor lamp filled with clear, viscous liquid in which a red ball was floating up and down. The ball was slowly sinking then blending into a similar red liquid at the bottom of the cylinder, almost as if they were creatures from outer space. Out of their communion a brilliant red creature was formed, morphing slowly into a ball shape and bobbing upward.

The man watched it for a long time.

A couple came up next to him, and the young woman asked her companion, "What's that? How does it work?"

"I think it's a matter of specific gravity. That floating part must be a substance whose specific gravity becomes lighter when heated up."

"What kind of substance, then?"

"That's beyond my knowledge."

"Weird, isn't it?"

The couple left, and other people stood next to him, had similar conversations, and left too.

The store was known for turning amateur inventors' ideas into commercial goods and bringing them to the market. The novelty floor lamp was a British product called a Phantom Light.

After looking at it a while longer, the man finally shook his head.

"There's no way I could create such a thing," he thought.

He left the store window and joined the crowd at the train station. Walking along with the crowd out of habit, he thought, "Humans are just like that red ball."

He came to the platform of a suburban railway. It was the start of the line and the train was packed, so he sat down on a bench to wait for the next train. He numbly watched the crowd running to the train and squeezing themselves into a car that was already packed with passengers.

"After all, I live a carefree life." As he muttered this, he felt something cold in his heart and was aware of being profoundly frustrated. "I envy people who can invent things like that cylindrical lamp."

He saw an unexpectedly beautiful sky next to the roof that covered the platform. It was too beautiful for a sky in the city.

He imagined an airship gliding through the sky—a yellow ship that floats as if in a fairy tale, a benevolent being that embraces him. At the same time, he thought of the man who put his heart and soul into bringing an airship over to Japan.

"I want to do something, too. I don't want to work for others anymore."

But, where on earth could he find such a job?

He dropped his finished cigarette and stepped on it.

When he turned his head, he saw a big, metal wastebasket. He bent down, picked up the flattened, dirty cigarette butt, stood up, and threw it in the basket.

"Enough about that," he thought. "I need to find a bur for Chie that still has chestnuts in it."

Since his daughter had found the chestnut tree, he had gone there with her a few times. The house had a garage with iron doors, and right behind the fence stood the big chestnut tree. It extended its branches over the fence, and the branches had many nuts. Several burs were on the ground in front of the garage, but every one was cracked and the brownish inside was bare. He and his daughter checked them one by one, but all the chestnuts had already been taken by someone.

"See? Everything is gone," the girl told him as if she had known this all along. She suggested, "We should come here very early in the morning. We need to come as soon as the wind blows."

"Yeah, you're right."

The man nodded and looked up at the big chestnut tree, which must have been quite old. There were many green burs on the branches but everything was too high on the tree. It would be impossible to get them even if he had a long stick.

Since then, the same thing kept happening to him. He was used to sleeping in late, and the house with the chestnut tree was in the opposite direction of her preschool, so every time he went there it was after the girl came home and all he ever found was the remains of the burs.

"Why is Chie so fascinated with chestnuts?" he was thinking in the back of his mind as he waited on the bench at the station.

Suddenly and unexpectedly, a very old recollection came back to him. He was a boy and giving his aged father a shoulder massage. The father's shoulder was bony and thin, and he could see deep wrinkles on his turned-down neck.

"When I was a child," the father said, as if listening carefully to the sound of a strong autumn wind that was causing trees to shake, "when a strong wind blew like now, chestnuts in the mountain behind our house fell off the tree and landed with a plop. I used to enjoy picking them up, putting them in a box, and counting how many I had."

The man could almost hear the voice of his father of his late years, which he had half-forgotten.

His father was from a rustic mountain village the man had never visited. Although the man had grown up and lived in the city all his life, the sound of chestnuts falling on the ground echoed in his ears so nostalgically, as if he had heard it before.

"This must have skipped a generation," the man mused. He gave it an oddly serious thought, then shook his head fretfully, thinking, "Nonsense. No use thinking of such things. I wish my brain were made in a way that I could invent something."

When he came to himself, the train he had been waiting for had arrived and was already so full of people that all the seats seemed to be occupied. He decided to wait for the next train one more time.

That night, as usual, the girl was in her little bed, talking to her doll and stroking it.

"Mister Chestnut, you must be so lonely being alone."

"Why don't I buy roasted sweet chestnuts for you, Chie?"

She answered her father with a serious look on her face: "No, I want real chestnuts, not the ones we eat."

After the girl fell asleep, the wife said to him, "She is so intrigued with chestnuts. Please get up early and bring some home. Unless you become the early bird, you'll never catch the worm, you know."

Although she said it jokingly, it was the very first request she had made to her husband, who moped around day after day while she said nothing.

Compliantly the man got up early on the following morning, took his daughter by the hand, and walked to the house with the chestnut tree. It was thirty minutes earlier than the time she usually left for preschool.

From the moment they left the house, the girl had been half-running, dragging him by the hand. But when they turned the corner of the street, she stopped dead.

There were three elementary school boys in front of the garage, hunkered down and cracking chestnut burs with a stone.

The girl just stood there and didn't walk any more.

"Chie, let's go ask them to give us a couple."

Despite the man's encouragement, she shook her head, kept a firm grasp on his hand, and just stared at what the boys were doing.

Soon, they carelessly stuffed the chestnuts into their pockets and ran off shouting to each other.

Then the girl took the initiative. She walked to the garage, and stared at the scattered debris as if she were critiquing it.

"Daddy, look around. You might be able to find one."

"You look with me."

"No, the burs sting me."

He flipped over some burs but, as expected, no chestnut was left.

"Not even one left, huh?" Unexpectedly the girl seemed to have resigned herself easily.

"Next time let's come back as soon as the wind blows," he said to the girl.

He went back to the apartment with his daughter and told his wife what had happened.

"It's really difficult to get chestnuts, isn't it?" The wife smiled. "Do you mind taking her to preschool now?"

"I'm tired. Sorry, but can you go, please?"

"You are no good," the wife said with a smile, but he sensed a hint of accusation in her voice.

While lying on his back alone in the six-mat room, he talked to himself as if he were regretting: "Chestnuts … Airship …"

In his mind, they were related and mingled in a subtle way. He spent a long time imagining shiny chestnuts coming out of fresh burs and dreaming about an airship slowly and freely floating.

"I choose an airship over a chestnut. I'm not a kid."

Even after his wife came home, he was still thinking about the man who was trying to bring an airship—what has happened since then to the plan that would cost two-hundred million yen and to the project whose staff he wanted to join?

Before noon, he wandered out and went down the slope he had walked so many times for so many years. The road was not wide and had recently become a one-way street. At the beginning it had seemed convenient for him, as no cars came from behind, but soon the amount of traffic increased and now he had to stop at the roadside to wait for the continuous stream of small trucks to pass.

There was a two-story house under construction on his way, and in front of it were a couple of housewives holding shopping bags as they stood talking with each other.

"This is going to be an apartment. But the street is supposed to be widened before too long, so building it here is a violation."

"Then they'll probably demand lots of compensation to remove it again—they are crafty, aren't they?"

Hearing this conversation that had nothing to do with him, he walked on, past a gas station that had also recently been built, and went into a public phone booth. He could have used the phone in the apartment, but it was in the building manager's office and he would have been overheard, so he preferred to walk all the way to the phone booth.

He thumbed through the phone book and checked the number of a newspaper company. If he remembered correctly, "The Man Who

Imports His Dream Airship" was in a magazine published by the newspaper company.

When his call was answered, he asked for the editorial department and inquired about the article. However, the office was busy and the article had been written a long time ago, so it went nowhere. Finally he got the information that the reporter who had handled the article was on a business trip and wouldn't be back to the office for three days.

"I'll call again then. Thank you," the man said.

"Excuse me, but may I ask who you are?" the person on the other end of the line asked near the end of the conversation.

"Uh, I'm an airplane or airship buff, so I was simply interested in the article." That was all he could say on the spur of the moment.

"Oh, I see." The person sounded bothered and roughly hung up the phone.

The man hung up as well and just stood in the phone booth for no reason. Finally he opened the door and stepped outside. While waiting for a few cars to pass on the street in front of him, he bitterly said to himself, "I really have too much free time."

His wife bought some chestnuts at a vegetable store for their daughter. They were big and beautiful, glossy and smooth.

Since the last time, the man had walked to the house with the chestnut tree several times, sometimes with the girl and sometimes alone. It was always disappointing, and some days he couldn't even find a bur. Perhaps the resident of the house promptly cleaned up all the burs.

"Look, Chie, aren't these beautiful chestnuts?" the wife said.

"Uh-huh."

The girl got down on her hands and knees and rolled them with her fingers. But she didn't seem as happy as expected, and she quickly got bored with rolling them.

"Chie, tell me the story of Mister Chestnut," the man cajoled, but she said brusquely, "The ghost of Mr. Chestnut … Please come, my bride … That's it—I forget the story."

The man watched a little TV and then suddenly stood up.

"I'm going out."

"Where to?" the wife asked.

"I'm going with you," the girl said.

"I have a little errand but I'll be back very soon. I'll play with you later."

The man hurriedly slipped on a pair of sandals, walked down past the apartment that was under construction, and went into his usual phone booth.

For the last few days, all he had done was to try to find out more about the plan to import the airship. He knew it was ridiculous, but he couldn't rest until he found out. Finally he had gotten hold of the reporter on the phone and gotten the number of the Japan Airship Organizing Office. The reporter hadn't contacted the office since the time he had written the article, so he encouraged the man to call the office directly if he was so interested in the latest news.

After the man dialed, a woman answered in a businesslike manner, "Yokozawa Corporation." She confirmed that the Airship Organizing Office was there, but the person in the office was always out. Whenever the man asked her when he would be back, she only said that she didn't know.

Today, however, the person—the man who was to bring the airship—was in. When the woman said, "Hold on, please," he felt his heart quicken. That surprised him—after all, this really had nothing to do with him.

The person came to the phone.

"Hello," the man said hesitantly, then hastily asked, "Are you the person who is in charge of the Airship Organizing Office?"

"Yes, I am."

"I'm calling because I read the article about the airship in a magazine. I'm fascinated by airships. When is it coming?"

"Well," the person said in a matter-of-fact voice, "it will be announced through a different organization. At some point, that organization will make a detailed announcement. Until then, I cannot say anything."

"But," the man carried on, "is it coming this year? Or will it be next year?"

"I'm not allowed to say."

The flat refusal made him feel betrayed. Now he quickly became despondent.

"I'm sorry to bother you."

He hung up the phone. As he left the booth, the wave of street noise overwhelmed him.

He plodded home, wondering why the person had given him such a dry response. Is he a promoter who has competitors? Does another organization really exist? No, no, I don't think so. The Airship Organizing Office probably has only one desk in the corner of a small trading company office, so perhaps he is hard-pressed for funds. He may not have any sponsors. The plan must have foundered and is going nowhere.

The man looked up at the sky. It was clear yet hazy, which was somewhat irritating. He didn't remember when, but he recalled seeing a more fairy tale–like and comforting sky. When he was a child, the sky always seemed to be like that.

The man tried to imagine the yellow ship floating in the sky, but to no avail.

He thought, "This is no longer a sky that the airship can float in. Nowhere, not even in my mind."

In the evening, his wife served boiled chestnuts after dinner. The big chestnuts were tender and sweet, and the girl ate them happily. But then she said, "I want real chestnuts."

"But these are real ones."

"I'm not talking about chestnuts that we eat. I'm talking about chestnuts in a bur."

"Oh, all chestnuts are in a bur. These were, too."

Even after hearing this explanation, the girl remained dissatisfied. She kept fingering five chestnuts that had been set aside.

When she went to her little mattress, she put these chestnuts next to her doll and said, "Mister Chestnut, I promise I'll pick up a prettier, real bride for you."

Later, after the man turned off the TV that he had been watching mindlessly, the wife reminded him, "You have an appointment with the unemployment office the day after tomorrow."

"Uh-huh," he nodded and said slowly. "I'll seriously look for a job this time."

"Oh, I didn't mean that. It's just that you seem to forget things these days."

"What do you mean I forget? I haven't been doing anything," the man responded.

"That's okay—everyone needs some time like that."

"You are a good wife," the man said quietly. "Chie is also a good daughter. Yet I'm doing nothing."

"Don't be so hard on yourself." The wife flashed her familiar smile. "Why don't you go to sleep?"

"Yeah, I am," the man replied in exhaustion.

"That wall calendar is too big and lurid," he thought. "I should change it."

When he woke up later that night, a strong wind was blowing outside and the windows were rattling. Listening carefully in the darkness, he could feel a storm-force wind blowing far away, shaking houses and trees.

When he woke up next, the wind was still blowing. Every time he woke up from his unpleasant sleep, the wind was continually blowing.

Chestnuts will fall. Surely many of them will, he thought, half-dreaming.

When he woke up next, the air was calm. The world that had been violently shaken was tranquil, and he could hear his wife's and daughter's faint breathing as they slept.

He turned on the bedside lamp and looked at the alarm clock: almost five o'clock.

The man got up and hurried into his clothes. Careful not to wake up his wife and daughter, he turned off the light and slipped out.

In the opalescent shade, everything was cool and serene. The cold air woke up his sleep-deprived brain, driving out the fogginess. He felt slightly excited for the first time in a long while, as if he were going to work. He walked briskly along the soundless street.

Leaves were scattered on the street. There were various leaves, not just yellowed and browned ones but even green ones, blown down by last night's wind.

"I bet a lot of chestnuts have fallen off the tree." he mused hopefully.

He strode eagerly around the last corner.

On the street in front of the garage were some fallen leaves but no chestnut burs. Frantically hunting around, he saw not even one empty bur. As he looked at the tree over the wall, a deep, bottomless disappointment came over him. All the burs that had been on the branches were now gone. No matter how carefully he scanned up and down, there were absolutely no burs, not even in the topmost branches.

The people in the house must have picked all the chestnuts off the tree yesterday before the windstorm. From the emptiness of the top branches, he figured they must have hired a workman.

The old chestnut tree with its thick leaves suddenly changed to an utterly empty, meaningless thing to him. The sky above the tree was finally turning bluish, presaging a sunny day, but that also felt meaningless.

A filthy white dog appeared from the corner, sniffed a power pole, and slunk down a side street.

"No chestnut, no airship …"

Once more he looked up at the brightening sky that he could no longer care about.

"It's about time I get a job."

Now weary again from lack of sleep, he thought, absentmindedly, "But I don't know what for."

ↀↀↀ

improper

Furin

不倫

□□□

There, too, was light—a faint phosphorescence emitted by lichens.

Finally Kuikui opened his mouth. His voice sounded hollow, like water oozing from the ground.

"Are you saying that you cannot kill her, no matter what?"

"I don't know," Kar mumbled. "I just don't know."

Kuikui, who is old, was sitting in the dimness on the opposite side, but Kar could make out his movement, his irritation. Behind Kuikui was total darkness. Everything, even the rock face, was hidden in blackness.

"You are sick," his hollow voice echoed in the dark.

"Probably so," Kar muttered.

"You don't know what you are saying."

"You are absolutely right." Then Kar raised his voice in disobedience, "But what's wrong with it?"

"It's wrong." The voice was very low, impenetrable to any objections. "That's how it has always been."

"Always been …" Kar shook his head again and again. "I don't understand. I really don't understand it."

"That's how it has always been. Nobody can change it."

"What if I do change it?"

"You cannot. If it were something you could change, someone would have done so a long time ago. Nobody has been able to."

"I hate it."

"Hate it as much as you want," he said coldly, "but if hatred were capable of moving it, it would have been moved already."

"It's not that I want to disrespect the convention. I just want to keep living with her."

"Why?"

"I would be lost without her."

"Nonsense," the voice said flatly. "You just feel that way. It's an illusion."

"I know," Kar said quietly, as if speaking to himself. "But I'm simply not going to kill her."

A short silence. The darkness quivered as the tentacles of the aged Kuikui trembled.

"If you don't," Kuikui said in a solemn tone, "you'll immediately be ostracized, and that's not all. The worst part is that you will bring harm to everyone."

"How so? How does it become everyone's issue?"

"It's because what you are trying to do is unthinkable. Nobody has ever done it before, and it will invite confusion and corruption."

"I don't understand."

"I think you do," Kuikui said in a softer, mentoring tone. "You know that as a male you are the one who has a future, who will leave the underground and move out of this darkness. That's not the case for a female. She will die soon and return to the soil and the darkness. There is no way a male and a female can stay together as husband and wife forever. Even to think it's possible is indecent. If you love her, you should have killed her a long time ago, as everyone does his wife."

"If I love her? Do you think that's what love is?"

"It's not for us to think. A male's responsibility is to have a female bear him a child. Then love is complete. If you kept the same woman as your wife forever, we'd all soon vanish."

"I want to vanish, then."

"You are out of your mind." His voice, brimming with anger, roared in Kar's ears. "And what about her? Naturally she desires to observe the convention, doesn't she? Your duty is to have dozens of females bear your children. Are you rejecting your duty and also her wishes?"

"I don't know." Kar lowered his head and held his tentacles close to his body.

"You do know. You must go to see her. Kill her immediately. Don't think, and your proper instincts will guide you. Now, go."

Kar didn't move. He was devastated, dropping his tentacles and collapsing on a dark rock. He could hear the water dripping in a corner of the dim cave.

"Go on. Don't think about anything," Kuikui encouraged him. "I'll be waiting for you. I won't tell anyone until then."

"I'm going." Kar began crawling. At the mouth of the cave, though, he shouted behind him, shaking with a rage that suddenly overcame him.

"I'm going to my wife. And I will never kill her—not in my lifetime!"

Kar crawled on, still shaking. The passage was filled with darkness. Just by the faint luminescence of the lichens he could see unmarried females all around, confined to pits in the rocks, crouching and crawling. What a tremendous number of females there were! The scene made Kar feel like vomiting. He did not see any males. It would be a long search in that subterranean passage to find even one male.

"What a destiny," Kar thought. All this suffering just because there are few males and many females. Females die sooner, and they bear only one child; most of the babies are female, too. It's true that the species will vanish if they don't follow the tradition. Nevertheless, could he kill his dear wife? Could he live without her? Suddenly he shuddered again. Racked with pain, he groaned in the darkness. He is only allowed to refer to his special female as "she" or "my wife," because females don't have names. When she is killed, she will be thrown away aboveground, to shrivel and eventually be reduced to sand. She will be lost forever. Nothing, absolutely nothing, will remain.

Well, then, what if he gives her a name? With a name, she would become a special being, an individual, distinguished from the other females. When she dies, he could call out her name, so that her never-changing figure would dwell forever in his memory. Yes, he should give her a name.

With this wild idea, he regained some composure. On the other hand, new anxieties emerged. In any event, it was good he didn't mention this to Kuikui. This must remain a secret between himself and her. He would call her by name, and keep her as his wife until her natural death took her away from him. She had already borne her child but, really, who on earth could kill her?

Before he knew it, Kar arrived at his own cave—a private abode allowed only to males. Only females who are wives can live there too, for that time.

Here also lichens were giving off a glimmer of light.

"Is it you?" said a thin voice that sounded both eager and bleak.

"It's me," Kar responded.

"It's you, right?" she asked again.

Kar crawled to her and studied her familiar body lying in the dim light.

She quietly stretched her tentacles and they interlaced with his. That feeling, because of its faintness, stung his skin and filled his heart with emotion. A mysterious peace and the suffering he had been experiencing mixed together inside him.

He softly caressed her, she with whom he had shared his life for some time. Her softness, warmth, and embrace will surely vanish like dew at some point, but could he hurry them into eternal nothingness by his own hand?

The two bodies intertwined and caressed each other for a while in the gloom.

"I love you," she whispered.

"I love you, too, Hea-Pea," he responded.

"Hea-Pea?"

"It's your name, Hea-Pea. And I love you."

He felt her stiffen.

"My name? The name for me?" In a tremulous voice, she said, "Who allowed you to give it to me? Who told you it's okay? It's not good."

"It's nobody's business. You are Hea-Pea, and I'd like to call you Hea-Pea from now on."

"It's not permitted."

"I don't care. I want to call you by your name. Do you understand, Hea-Pea?"

"Stop it!" she shouted. "I'm scared."

"Why, Hea-Pea?"

"Please stop it. I'm begging you."

Kar was taken aback, baffled, feeling her body going rigid. He did not understand why she had to act like that. He slowly extended his tentacles and softly rubbed her. When she stopped shaking, he said, "It's okay, I won't use your name any more. But tell me why you don't want me to."

"Because …" her body went rigid again just uttering the words, "because it's a bad thing to do."

"I see," he sighed. "It's because this has been decided upon, right?"

"Kar, I love you."

The two kept silent a while, touching each other's tentacles.

She told him, "Thanks to you, I've been happy, living with you, loved by you, and bearing your child. But …"

"But?"

"Kar, I'm so afraid"—she held him tightly in her tentacles—"because you keep putting off killing me."

"You, listen carefully," Kar said. "You will die before I do, and we cannot help that. But you must be here until you die in my arms naturally. Why should I kill you while you are living?"

"But that has been decided and I accept it."

"I don't," Kar insisted. "As long as we love each other, the convention means nothing. This is nobody's business but ours." He asked, "Do you really love me?"

"Yes," she said painfully.

"And I love you, too. I want to be with you as long as you're alive. I'd like you to be my wife until your time comes."

"That can't work. I've already borne my child, you know."

"That's no problem. What matters is you."

"Kar!" she shouted. "I love you more than anything, even more than our mother darkness. But if you love me, please grant my wish!"

"Are you asking me to kill you?"

She was silent.

"I cannot," Kar groaned. "Are you so very afraid of continuing to be with me?"

"I'm delighted to be with you, but I'm afraid because it's forbidden."

"Who forbids it? I know, everyone forbids it. But I say, if our love is strong, we can change this."

"We shouldn't."

"Why not? Really, why not? Because it's a convention?"

"No, the convention is just a form. But there is something real behind it. I cannot explain it, and you probably can't understand. But something is there."

"Aren't you afraid of dying?"

"No, because it's meant to be, and because I'll be killed by you who love me."

"I cannot kill you."

They turned their faces away from each other. Lichens were glowing, water dripping faintly.

Kar could not comprehend. He was outraged. Male and female are different, but why must they be so tragically different? He could accept the differences between himself and Kuikui or others, but it was unbearable to think that he and Hea-Pea were worlds apart.

Filled with icy sorrow, he held her, moaning.

When he regained consciousness—he had been delirious for a while—he found that he was wringing her neck. Following the convention, he had wrapped three tentacles together and was choking her. She barely struggled, suffered a little, and then became still. Absent-mindedly he looked at his wife's immobile body. He softly caressed its skin and touched its tentacles. Already the skin was losing its warmth and the tentacles dangling. Yes, she was dead. He had killed her.

He crouched near the corpse for a long time without stirring. Then he wept silently. But what good was groaning or crying? Behind him, he heard the dripping water again.

Kar jerked himself awake. He knew he must dispose of his wife's body.

He lifted her onto his back. She was unexpectedly light, and he could feel her remaining body temperature on his skin. When he began crawling, her thin tentacles swung in the air.

He crawled out of the cave and kept going through the underground passage. Numerous females silently flattened themselves into every crevice in the rocks, watching Kar carrying his dead wife on his back. Some areas in the passage were completely dark, and he had to make his way by extending his tentacles ahead of him. In other areas, mounds of iridescent moss cast shadows upon wet bare rocks and the many females cowering in their holes. He straightened his wife's light body on his back and kept crawling. Sometimes her dangling tentacles got in his way; they were cold and limp, and each time he lifted them they fell back down.

The passage was approaching the surface now. Kar could sense it in the subtle change of temperature and soil.

Suddenly he heard a voice calling from behind.

He looked back and discerned the silhouette of Kuikui, sitting in a shadow that was darker than the darkness. Kuikui's tone suggested his deep relief and compassion. "Kar, you finally killed her."

Kar neither spoke nor moved.

"Well done," Kuikui continued in his dull, rusty voice. "It must have been hard for you."

Kar, still silent, hugged his wife's corpse in his six tentacles.

"You gave me a difficult time, Kar. But you'll soon forget about her, and you'll be able to perform more easily next time."

"Enough," Kar said. "Please be quiet."

"Go ahead," said Kuikui. "It's good that the upper world is in night now. Give her a good burial." He added, "Kar, I'm glad you killed her. If you hadn't, I would have had to kill you."

Kuikui turned his body slowly, and the darkness swallowed the old male as he left.

Kar carried on, through the long, winding underground tunnel that led to the upper world. Exchanging a few words with Kuikui had somehow brought him back from his emptiness, and he crawled onward with tears in his eyes.

It was night in the upper world—Kuikui was right. Even so, the shining stars were painfully bright to Kar's eyes, which were accustomed to the darkness of the underground. If it were not night, or if it were the time when the Fire Star occupies the sky, he wouldn't have been able to keep his eyes open. In the distance, there rose a black rocky mountain, and between it and the underground exit lay a stretch of desert. Only rolling sand dunes, where not even lichens grew, were stretched out in all directions under the starlight.

Kar laid his wife's body on the sand, and then, grasping her by the tentacles, he began tugging. It has been specified that a male must dust his wife's dead body with sand before abandoning it.

He occasionally bumped into roundish lumps of sand. These were abandoned female corpses from a long time ago. They would eventually dry out completely and vanish with the sandstorms.

He noticed alongside him the silhouette of another moving figure. The silhouette dragged a corpse for a short spell, then dumped it and disappeared back underground.

Kar, on the other hand, dragged his wife's body for a long time. Her tentacles that he was grasping were cold and didn't feel like hers. Turning his head, he saw that her body was so completely covered with sand that he could no longer recognize the features he used to cherish. Still he kept moving, the tears still seeping from his eyes.

At last he laid his wife's body down in the shade of a high sand dune. The corpse was so powdered with sand that it was shapeless. He began digging with his tentacles. It was difficult, because the dry sand kept sifting back into the hole. In tears, he persisted. Next he put his wife's corpse into the hole and covered it with sand. Everything, absolutely everything had vanished. He picked up a few rocks and arranged them in a circle. Nobody had ever done such a thing. It was lucky nobody was watching him. Even as he did it, he wondered what good his markers would do, as a sand storm would sweep everything away sooner or later.

He crouched near the circle of little stones for a long time, repeating in a low voice, "Hea-Pea. My Hea-Pea."

Nobody would rebuke him for calling his wife's name out here. Hea-Pea was in the sand pit now, but when he called her name, she was in his voice.

Tired of calling her name many times, he lay down on the sand. He knew he must go back to the underground and make a female his new wife.

But he did not want to go back.

He contemplated the vast, undulating desert below the magnificent, star-studded sky. The stars were twinkling and trembling as if they were talking to him. One of the moons shone dully near the horizon but the other one was not there. Kar stared at strings of stars and their strong and weak light. Long ago it was said that females who died would go to the stars. In the middle of the sky, his eyes fixed on one white star that was shining brightly. It was familiar to him—if he was right, it was the third child of the Fire Star. According to the elders, there are creatures there just like Kar, Kuikui, and Hea-Pea who are able to freely communicate their will and capable of complex thought.

Kar briefly pondered whether these creatures, seeing a fellow creature on a distant star who loves only one female throughout her life, would criticize him for forbidden and shameful behavior.

He cast his eyes down again to the ground. There on the sand sat a ring of unremarkable little rocks.

in the hollow

Utsuro no naka

うつろの中

♓♓♓

Deep darkness. Total black. No hint of even the dimmest light.

A voice: "Shall we keep waiting here?"

Another voice responds, "Be patient. We made it inside. Now we need to assess the situation."

Now a third voice speaks. "This is just a plant, and it's surrounded by the same species. They don't have any consciousness."

"Is there any species that has consciousness?"

"I'm detecting a slight wave but it's not quite consciousness. This seems to be a lower organism."

"It's not Myū, is it?"

"No. The Myū are much bigger. Also the Myū mental wave would be a little more complicated."

"You really overestimate the Myū," the first voice says. "In my opinion, there's no need for all this caution."

"But the Myū do have a certain civilization. They grow plants and use several different animals. Their colony is the product of a certain type of technology."

"Sure, technology of no importance or value."

"Let's not judge yet," interrupts another voice. "Remember we are scouts. We're here to investigate whether the Myū possess advanced intelligence or are primitive creatures."

"Hasn't it been obvious from simply observing them from high altitude?" a voice says disgustedly. "What are we wasting our time for?"

"Did you forget the three-legged aliens on Planet Caritana? They completely fooled us. They knew from the beginning that we were spying on them and were quite skillful at hiding their civilization from us. Remember the losses we suffered when our main troops landed there?"

"I'm telling you, the Myū don't have such abilities. According to our high-altitude surveillance, they don't possess even the most primitive form of power. I don't think …"

"Shut up. We need to focus on carrying out the duty assigned to us."

"That's right, so why are we just waiting here doing nothing?"

"What do you want to do?"

"If we've landed in our target zone, then there are supposed to be a number of habitats for the Myū here. We can take on their form and slip quietly into their population."

"Too dangerous. That might work in a big colony, but in a place like this where not many Myū live, a newcomer would attract their attention. And we still don't know if they have any telepathic powers."

"So?"

"So it would be better to disguise ourselves as a plant or as some form of the livestock they keep. We need to get close, in order to investigate their mental structure."

"Shhh!" a voice interrupts. "Something is coming. It's an animal. It could be a Myū."

"How many?"

"Two. Let's use our telepathy and enter their consciousness."

Silence. Pitch darkness. Footsteps approaching from afar, then silence again. The dark hollow fills with an air of relief, and the conversation resumes, without the need for any utterance.

"Extremely simple—their mental structure is totally unsophisticated. They don't have telepathic ability, either. Wow, I can see everything about them. Now I'm investigating below their level of consciousness … Ah, it's very simple, too—clear as day."

"Right? Didn't I tell you? We don't need to be so cautious with them."

"Not so fast. We must fulfill our mission to examine their life, their social patterns, and so on … Good, I'm detecting a desire in those two Myū. They are an elderly male and female. There is a good way of gaining entry into their home."

"How? Oh, I see. All right, let's do it."

"Then hurry up. We'll unite and morph into the thing they desire most."

"But do you think they'll even notice where we are?"

"Well, it's true they are dim and slow. Extremely simplistic. We might need to make some sound. Or, wait, let's emit some light—that will help them find us."

Through the bamboo grove come an elderly man and woman, who are referred to as Myū by their secret visitors.

"Oh, what is that? Look, something is shining over there."

"Oh, yes. A light! Hmmm, the big stalk of bamboo over there is shining."

"What do you think it is? Do you think something bad will …"

"Wait, wait. Let's cut it open. Oh, look at this!"

The old couple stands agape in astonishment. What appears from the big bamboo stalk is a baby girl, as beautiful as a fairy from their sweetest dreams.

After her amazement subsides at last, the old woman says, "She must be a gift from the gods. Let's raise her as best we can as our very own daughter."[1]

♓♓♓

---

1. The last paragraph of the story corresponds to the beginning of the well-known Japanese folktale *The Tale of a Bamboo Cutter* (*Taketori monogatari* 竹取物語).

my mother's cooking

Haha no aji

母の味

Editors frequently send me requests for essays about my mother's home cooking. I always turn them down. My mother was entirely too strange to ever have "mother's recipes" in the conventional sense.

When asked to describe the food my mother made, I'm at a loss. Until the end of the Second World War, she never even boiled rice. When all the maids left and she had to cook rice on her own, everyone was astounded that she was able to do it.

There is no doubt that my mother was raised as the beloved and spoiled daughter of a rich family, and that she grew into a woman of extravagant tastes. That said, she did have an inner fortitude. And in the years of deprivation immediately after the war, she was the one in our family who most cheerfully endured awful food and shabby clothing.

At present she is seventy years old. She still uses the subway and other public transportation and will not get into a taxi, in part because she's cheap but also, as she explains, because she wants to keep up the strength in her legs and hips. When I call for a taxi to go on a small errand, she'll scold, "A young man like you shouldn't be so bloody lazy."

Recently, my mother went on a package tour of the Middle East and Africa. Uncharacteristically she asked me to accompany her, and since there's no denying that she's elderly, I agreed to go along, for the first time in a long time.

Apparently she still considered me a schoolboy, for on boarding the airplane she took her seat quickly and called me over: "Hurry up! Come sit here. You'll be able to look out the window."

Upon our arrival, she instructed me to use the public restroom in the airport because there was no attendant so I wouldn't have to leave a tip.

At the hotel, she advised me, "They have chilled water here. Make sure you drink your fill." She also warned me repeatedly, "You drink and smoke too much." Going through customs between countries, she lectured, "You're going to have to tip everybody. So exchange some of your bills for coins now, while you can." She was a veritable font of detailed and trivial advice.

I am a middle-aged man with experience in traveling. But parents will be parents, and there was nothing I could do but meekly accept her suggestions.

The most difficult problem in sharing a room with my mother was my nightcap before bed. Most hotels provide two glasses. It was my custom to mix a very strong whisky highball in one, put iced water in the other, and drink from them alternately. In our room I was certain there had been two glasses, but I could only find one. I finally discovered why when I came upon the creepy vision of my mother's dentures soaking in the missing glass.

My mother took it upon herself to bathe first and then tell me, "I filled the bathtub for you. Please hurry and take your bath." But the bath she drew was always too hot or too cold, and I could never get into the water without considerable adjustment of the temperature.

On one occasion, my mother called, "There is no bath towel in here," and she came flying out of the bathroom almost naked. I like women, but I was far from delighted to see a strip show put on by my seventy-year-old mother.

One thing my mother wasn't good at was unlocking the hotel room door. On one occasion our door had a double lock, and even I was having trouble opening it, whereupon my mother suddenly grabbed hold of a foreign gentleman who was passing by in the corridor. He was not an employee but a guest, yet she sternly commanded, "Open this door."

My intention had been to help my mother on her journey, but it turned out that I was the one constantly receiving my mother's assistance. She never once got sick. Indeed, she was incredibly healthy and active throughout the trip. On days of scheduled activities, I was the one who got tired out. We frequently woke up at five in the morning, and since it was my usual custom to sleep until noon, the schedule was agonizing.

At the end of a day of sightseeing, I collapsed in exhaustion on the bed, and my mother turned to me and said nonchalantly, "I feel the end of my life is soon approaching, and before I go I want to visit the South Pole."

on layabouts

Namakemono ron

なまけもの論

Women complain that men are overbearing. Men counter that they have a job to do. "Job" is the word men use for a multitude of excuses. We've all seen a "big man" who has his wife put a tie around his neck, line up his shoes and put his feet into them, and hand him his briefcase. Then, in perfect seriousness, he says, "We men have to face so many enemies once we leave the house." Out he walks, arrogantly throwing back his head—only to slip on a banana peel and fall flat on his back. At this, he looks back fiercely at his wife and says, "See? I told you!" He groans and then walks off, his ego still unbruised. The fact is, such men tend to be useless at their actual jobs, spending half their time removing their nose hairs and lining them up on their desks.

Women may be delighted to read the above, but in reality it's not an easy dilemma to solve. To begin with, how many men have actually slipped on a banana peel in modern times, although some might have in the distant past? Because of numerous depictions of slipping on a banana peel in stories and cartoons, the danger of the banana peel was exaggerated and so we have become overly sensitized to banana peels. Actually, if a man did slip and was injured because of a banana peel, it would surely make headlines, probably not on the front page but in a social column.

Leaving aside the problem of banana peels, the word "job" used by men is a ridiculous cliché. The grander adjective it has, such as a "noble" profession or "heroic" labor, the farther it deviates from our true biological needs, which are food, clothing, and shelter. Consider, for example, a man who goes out to chop down trees with an ax to build a hut. It requires strength to use an ax, so he builds up his arm muscles by lifting up a rock. Another man passes by and lifts up a heavier rock. So the first man, showing anger, responds by hoisting an even heavier rock. Then more men gather and join the competition. Completely ignoring the cutting of trees, the man spends all day vying to lift the heaviest rocks.

Eventually he raises a rock as big as a small mountain, lifting it up above eye level, but the ground is so soft that he sinks in gradually, and the huge rock now covers the spot where he sank. Alas, the man comes to an end. People carve on the rock "The Grave of the Hero," clap their hands, and praise his great strength. Nobody pays any attention to his wife crying and screaming.

Men are enticed into doing various things by questionable passion. Most of the time, it has nothing to do with meeting our fundamental needs for survival.

Or take another example: There is a road that goes through the peak of a high mountain. One day, looking at the road, a man slaps his knee with a gleam in his eye. He gets a hammer and chisel from his house, and begins to cut a tunnel through the hard rock. He doesn't go home even to eat or sleep. His beard grows long and matted, and his cheeks and eyes become sunken, but he keeps digging. Finally his wife leaves home with the kids, and his house becomes dilapidated, with weeds growing over it. He doesn't care. He's forgotten that he began chiseling the tunnel for the benefit of his fellow villagers; now the act of digging itself has become an obsession. More than ten years pass, and finally the long tunnel is completed. As bright sunlight shines through from the other side, the shriveled man, who looks like a mummy, nods with satisfaction and keels over dead.

The villagers—who used to ridicule him and call him a wacko, vagabond, or mole—assemble to praise him as a hero, benefactor, and pioneer. They name the tunnel "Mole Tunnel" and he becomes a revered local legend. In this case, even if his family has broken up, the more misery his family has experienced because of his action, the more honors he would receive.

As a far less grand example, let's talk about a particular writer. His wife comes back from the beauty salon and wants him to admire her new hairdo, but he doesn't even bother to look at her. When she tells him that she made tea for him, he grunts "uh-huh," and when she reports that their child has failed in school, he murmurs that the child has inherited his genes. In the worse case, he might as well be yelling at her, "Get lost!" Yet he applies plenty of passionate engagement to his own job. In fact, he tears out his hair just trying to decide whether this or that sentence should use "I am" or "I'm."

After his struggles, his work turns out to be a masterpiece (actually, it usually isn't, but let's say it is for our convenience) that will be a literary classic for all posterity. Does the world benefit from this masterpiece? I seriously doubt it. Even if it somehow improves the world in a broader sense, the phrase over which the writer ripped out his hair has no effect on the average reader. It's like a piece of music that is understood only by a trained musicologist.

It would be better for the world if the writer took an interest in his wife's new hairdo and wrote merely a semi-masterpiece. Readers who can distinguish a masterpiece from a semi-masterpiece might think that the masterpiece would enrich their lives, but those people tend either to get depressed by masterpieces or to become writers themselves who rip out their hair over the choice of "I am" or "I'm." Therefore, I calculate that a masterpiece may do more harm than good. Roughly speaking, a man's job is generally like that.

By contrast, a woman's work better serves her biological nature and the survival of humankind. Lately fewer women are doing this sort of work, but that's due to changes in society, not in women per se.

Honeybees clearly exemplify the difference between men's and women's jobs. A queen bee, as we know, plays the fundamentally important role of laying eggs. Worker bees fly around gathering honey, build hives, and take care of baby bees. They are females, too, although they are atrophied and sterile. On the other hand, drones, who are the male honeybees, are truly lazy and incompetent dullards who basically do nothing. They enjoy sunbathing and goofing off, which makes them seem enviable to male humans, but soon they are driven out of the hives and starve to death. They reap what they sow, but it is a pitiful, miserable end.

Among humans, too, females' work is much more important than males' as far as the survival of humanity is concerned. Females diligently cook for others and breastfeed babies. In addition, from a male point of view, women have elegant figures, sweet voices, and tender hearts (actually, there are many females who don't, but let's say they do for our convenience). In short, a woman works in accordance with nature, whereas a man often does things that go against nature.

Even with women, though, if the work goes too far, it begins to transform into a "job." By nature, a woman attracts a man with her smooth, slender legs and soft, beautiful hair, makes a love nest with him, and lives happily ever after. But too often, a woman works overtime to make her natural assets even more effective. To make her legs look even longer, she wears high heels, but they are unhealthier than Tengu's single-tooth sandals and may cause a miscarriage.[1] She also heats and electrifies her lovely hair to make it curly. They are no longer considered her natural efforts to catch a man nor a manifestation of her rivalry against other women: they are excessive, strange obsessions.

The same can be said about running a kitchen. She studies culinary art and learns all possible cooking styles on earth through television programs and cookbooks. Because of her efforts, the human race

---

1. *Tengu* 天狗 are long-nosed legendary creatures and are commonly depicted wearing *geta* 下駄, traditional Japanese footwear that look similar to flip-flops. *Geta* normally have two supporting wooden blocks underneath called *ha* 歯 (teeth), but *Tengu* wear *geta* that only have a single-tooth.

will keep thriving. But if she gets a little overenthusiastic, then it becomes a job. If a man tries to drink milk from the bottle, the woman slaps his hand and pours the milk into a glass for him. A man has to obey her in this case, because drinking from a glass is a more civilized way and better for digestion.

However, say she decides to make a dish that requires an enormous amount of time and effort, like building an Egyptian pyramid. When this happens, you wouldn't know when the cooking will be done. When you think it's about time to eat, the dish is only half-cooked. She painstakingly arranges it on the plate according to the law of the golden ratio, and then rearranges it for color or some other esthetic effect. She garnishes it with an elaborately carved apple, saying, "It looks like a bunny, doesn't it?" An apple tastes the best when we take bites out of a whole one! After making you wait for half a century, she smiles and declares the dinner ready, by which time you've died of starvation.

But in short, this is what a woman's job is like. Of course, to fully explicate the essential qualities of women, I'd need to delve into female psychology, and that's a voluminous thesis that I won't get into here.

As we have seen, there is an essential difference between men's and women's jobs. Both jobs are dignified, solemn, and worthy of respect, yet both tend to do more harm than good to the human race. In my opinion, both men and women work too diligently and enthusiastically. But when they do so, that disparity gets wider and wider until men no longer understand women and women no longer understand men. If they both were less motivated and more idle, there would be a lot fewer misunderstandings, conflicts, complaints, and grudges between men and women.

I truly respect jobs, but humans work too hard. They work breathlessly with bloodshot eyes, which is not the right way. One psychologist compared our lives to a marathon race: because others get caught up in running, we feel pressured and begin running as well, most of us not knowing the purpose of the race but simply running because that's what others are doing. If you paused to rest, people would call you a dropout or a layabout, and you would be labeled a loser. In my view, it might be more humanlike if we did slow down, to gaze at the clouds or to catch snails and sing them a song. "Layabout" shouldn't be an insult, but an accolade. At least we feel some sort of affinity with the word "layabout." It's because being a layabout is so like a human—after all, playfulness and laziness are quintessential characteristics of being human. And certainly nobody works hard in the paradise or heaven that ancient people fantasized about. There, play and work blend together.

I realize there are rich and poor, kings and slaves, lands where crops are abundant and lands where people need to pick up shell fragments rather than a plow, so it might sound imprudent to encourage people to goof off and be lazy. But to consider such activities imprudent is itself a fallacy. At least, as a first step, everyone—rich or poor, talented or untalented—should try to be a layabout within their own means. In my opinion, it is the ideal for humans.

As a species, we humans have been fearless workaholics. Humans have worked so hard that we rose above all the other creatures on the planet. However, I wonder if this is something that we can be proud of. Our world has been developed thanks to intrepid explorers who risked their lives—I cannot read their diaries without weeping. But is it good or necessary for us and our world to have developed so quickly? Scientists have landed a rocket on the moon, and now space travel, which people have dreamed about since ancient times, could soon become a reality; however, if we hadn't been able to land on the moon, we could still have those dreams and enjoy our imagination. Don't get me wrong: I'd be the first person to buy a ticket into outer space. For many years I've wanted to be an explorer, so I climbed a mountain to build up my physique, read a book on astronomy, studied natural history, obtained a physician's license, learned to shoot a gun and drive a car, and wrote a book (though it's lousy) in preparation for writing an expedition record. So I'm not making an argument opposed to striving for progress.

We are blessed with an exceptional civilization thanks to our hardworking ancestors, yet still we work like a wild pig whose tail is on fire, or like a drunkard crazed with absinthe. We have lost sight of the objective of our jobs. Even though we live in a world that would seem magical to ancient people, much of our so-called advancement is a hollow deceit. Let's think about what is most important for us humans: have we added more wisdom—not just knowledge, but wisdom—to the heritage that our ancestors left us?

We need to reconsider what a job really is. When a man carving a tunnel through a mountain tries to finish the work by sacrificing everything he has, it's the most human yet the least humane act. If you want to drill a tunnel, just drill ten feet and that's enough. Someone else will dig the next ten feet. Even if you tell everyone not to, someone will do it. It's human nature, and it's the same with scholarship and any other undertaking.

Let's spend our energy not in working so hard but in passionately cultivating our expertise at being a layabout. A layabout has time for vaguely pondering why this or that happens, or for absently caressing a partner. If everyone were a layabout like this, the world would be a more humane place to live.

I must admit I intended to write something different regarding men and women, but I got too excited while writing this, and so my original goal ceased to matter. It's not good to get carried away like this. If I'm not careful, I could get so revved up that I would start a movement to *layabout-ify* the whole world, gather signatures, and advocate for my cause day and night. Instead, I hastily vow to become a layabout myself and stop thinking of such intensive endeavors. So I end this draft here. Just one last note: I freely acknowledge that this whole essay is no more plausible than slipping on a banana peel.

♦♦♦

the red ghost and the white ghost

Akai obake to shiroi obake

赤いオバケと白いオバケ

Do you know a place called Aoyama Cemetery?

It is a large cemetery in Aoyama, Tokyo. I grew up in a house right next to it. When I was a child, I thought the cemetery was much, much bigger than it is now. It seemed endless. Of course, the size of the cemetery has not changed; rather, it appeared vast from my perspective as a child.

There was a song about it:

From Aoyama Cemetery
Three white ghosts, three
Three red ghosts, three
And after them came
a boy student in *hakama*[1]
jumping out of his clothes

---

1. *Hakama* is a type of traditional Japanese clothing, a skirtlike pants and worn with a kimono.

When we little kids sang this song, the cemetery seemed even scarier. It had many old, enormous trees, so even during the daytime it was shadowy and dim. The cemetery was not only inhabited by Red and White Ghosts, but also by Blue Ghosts and Purple Ghosts, spooks, monsters, one-eyed goblins, giants, and fifty-five thousand five hundred fifty-five foxes and badgers, or so it seemed to us children. These malevolent creatures resided behind every tombstone and in the cavities of ancient, moss-covered trees.

Eventually we grew from little kids to medium-sized kids, and from medium-sized kids to big kids. As we grew older, sixty-six thousand six hundred sixty-six scary ghosts and evil spirits dwindled to about three thousand, then to three hundred, then to thirty, then to only three, and at last they totally disappeared.

How silly we were. There were never any ghosts there at all, we said to each other.

Yet, there were still ghosts after all: one Red Ghost and one White Ghost remained. Both these creatures were small and not very scary. Or perhaps we shouldn't say "creatures" but rather "individuals," since they spoke in human language.

The two ghosts were grumbling to each other behind a tombstone.

"Times are not good," said the Red Ghost. "In the past, human beings were frightened of us. Little children were too scared to come into the cemetery in the evening. When we did find a child in the cemetery after dark, I would show the top of my head or the end of my tail, and the kid would fall down, jump up, and flee, dropping his baked yam or candy in his haste to get away."

"It wasn't just children," the White Ghost declared indignantly. "Even grown-ups were afraid of us. But then the schools taught everyone that there were no such things as ghosts. Now we're unemployed!"

"If things go on as they are, there'll be no reason for us to be here," observed the Red Ghost. "We're going to have to frighten these humans in a big way," he said, folding his arms defiantly across his chest.

"But even if we show ourselves, they won't believe we're ghosts.

They'd probably think we are just odd-shaped balloons or old cloths thrown away on the street."

"This is the age of commercialism," said the White Ghost excitedly. "We could advertise ourselves in some sensational way."

"That's right! We'll show these humans that we're for real." The two ghosts began to feel more confident.

They took out the heirlooms of their ancestors that they had hidden in the cavity of a tree. These were things like tops and marbles that children had lost, and old coins—one *sen,* five *sen,* and ten *sen.*[2] There were also gold and silver. Because these treasures had been passed down from generation to generation for thousands of years, they consisted of all kinds of things.

The two ghosts, with the money they had, hired a band of ten street musicians who were dressed as clowns, and they rented a convertible. They hung a banner on the car and paraded with their band of musicians down the main avenue of Tokyo.

Doo-dee-doo, boom-boom … what raucous and stirring music the band made!

The two ghosts rode in the convertible's front seat and twisted their heads around and waved their tails.

A noisy crowd of people gathered, wondering what this commotion was all about.

"Hey, you, what is this parade for?" One gentleman asked a clown in the band.

"We have no idea," the clown replied. "Ask the strange-looking ones in the convertible."

The gentleman ran alongside the convertible and shouted, "What in heaven are you two?"

"I'm a ghost," the Red Ghost replied, trying to sound as frightening as possible.

"That's right," the White Ghost added. "Me, too."

---

2. A *sen* 銭, a monetary unit in use until 1953, was equal to 1/100 of a yen.

"Well, Mr. Ghosts," the gentleman said, not seeming the least bit frightened, "you appear to be most amusing characters."

"We can change our appearance," the Red Ghost replied. "We can stretch ourselves out and shrink at will. What about that? Pretty scary, huh?"

"I'm not scared. I think you are just amazing!" the gentleman said, clapping his hands. "Will both of you sign a contract with me?"

"What?" The two ghosts exclaimed in unison.

"A contract. This is what I do," and the gentleman handed them his business card, which said "Advertising Bureau Chief, Red and White Brand Bubble Gum Company, Ltd."

"We'd love for you to go on television for us. Your colors are just right. And if you can stretch and shrink yourselves, that's perfect!"

The Red Ghost and the White Ghost turned around and began whispering to each other.

"What kind of deal is this?" said one.

"Well, we must keep up with the times," replied the other. "If we go on television, the entire country will learn about us. It's the best advertisement in the world."

"All right, then. Let's give it a try."

And thus it came to pass, the two ghosts appeared in a TV commercial for Red and White Bubble Gum. The two ghosts popped some gum in their mouths, chewed and blew bubbles, and also expanded themselves like balloons.

The commercial was a big hit, and the company changed its name to Ghost Brand Bubble Gum. Children would gather in front of the TV, waiting eagerly for the commercial. Then came its jingle:

Ghosts, ghosts, our dear ghosts,
Stretch, stretch, more and more
They grow as big and roly-poly as they wish
How wonderful it is!
Ghost Brand Bubble Gum

"How enchanting! What cute ghosts they are!" viewers exclaimed.

A flood of fan letters came in with comments such as "My beloved little ghosts, I cannot sleep at night if I don't see you on television," or "Dear Red Ghost, you are so cute when you flip your tail! I am ecstatic. Let me visit you." Every day fifty-five thousand five hundred fifty-five fan letters were delivered to the Red Ghost and the White Ghost.

In the beginning, as anyone would, they relished being so popular and celebrated. Still, they were ghosts, and they began to feel guilty for not scaring people and for being treated so nicely.

The ghosts grew rich and lived in a big apartment with an electric heater, a TV, a stereo, and other things. They now slept in a comfortable bed instead of the cemetery's thickets and tree hollows.

One night they were sleeping peacefully in bed, when they awoke suddenly with a heavy weight on their chests. Their room was in total darkness. Corpse candles began flickering here and there, and an unpleasant wind that smelled like blood blew through the room.

"What is that?"

Terrified, the two ghosts clutched each other tight. Suddenly something like a shadow appeared from nowhere.

"Eek! It's a ghost!" the Red Ghost screamed. The White Ghost was also trembling like a leaf. Then there came a very spooky voice: "You insolent ones have forgotten your mission as ghosts. Shame on you! You will pay for this."

The ghosts could hear the clanking of chains and the growls of supernatural beasts. Then in the dim light there appeared ghosts so scary that anyone would faint at the sight of them. There were Japanese ghosts, Chinese ghosts, Western and Afghani ghosts, and all sorts of other ghosts who glared with terrifying glittering eyes at the Red Ghost and the White Ghost.

"I'm scared, I'm scared!"

The two ghosts hugged each other and trembled all through the long night.

Since then, the two ghosts have not appeared before even one living human being. The bubble gum company looked high and low for them, hiring an army of searchers—a total of ninety-nine thousand nine hundred ninety-nine police officers, private detectives, and idle curiosity seekers—but the ghosts were not to be found.

They must have repented their former ways and gone into training on how to frighten people. So where are they now? I think they're back in Aoyama Cemetery, hiding behind this tombstone or that tree cavity. If you go looking for the Red Ghost and the White Ghost, you just might find them. But I must warn you: if they ever come out again, this time they might be really, really scary.

bibliography

Akiyama Shun. "'*Yūrei*' to '*Manbō*' no tairitsu." In *Kita Morio no sekai*, 138–141. Tokyo: Shinpyōsha, 1979.

Cabinet Office, Government of Japan. "Kunshō no juyo kijun." Last modified December 26, 2006. http://www8.cao.go.jp/shokun/seidokaikaku/juyokijun.pdf

Cohn, Joel R. *Studies in the Comic Spirit in Modern Japanese Fiction*. Cambridge: Harvard University Asia Center, 1998.

Fowler, Edward. *The Rhetoric of Confession: Shishōsetsu in Early Twentieth-Century Japanese Fiction*. Berkeley: University of California Press, 1988.

Hara Shirō and Mori Reiko. "Kita Morio to 'Bungei Shuto.'" In *Kita Morio no sekai*, 122–135. Tokyo: Shinpyōsha, 1979.

Hasegawa Izumi. *Sengo bungakushi*. Tokyo: Meiji Shoin, 1974.

Hijiya-Kirschmerit, Irmela. *Rituals of Self-Revelation: Shishōsetsu as Literary Genre and Socio-Cultural Phenomenon*. Cambridge: Harvard University Press, 1996.

Kita Morio. *Doctor Manbo at Sea*. Translated by Ralph F. McCarthy. Tokyo: Kōdansha International, 1987. Originally published as *Dokutoru manbō kōkaiki* (Tokyo: Chūō Kōronsha, 1960).

———. *Dokutoru Manbō kaisōki*. Tokyo: Nihon Keizai Shinbun Shuppansha, 2007.

———. *Dokutoru Manbō kōkaiki*. Tokyo: Chūō Kōronsha, 1960.

———. *Dokutoru Manbō konchūki*. Tokyo: Chūō Kōronsha, 1961.

———. *Dokutoru Manbō seishunki*. Tokyo: Chūō Kōronsha, 1968.

———. "Gōman to tōkai." In *Sono Ayako, Kita Morio,* by Sono Ayako and Kita Morio, 472–478. Vol. 16 of *De Luxe warera no bungaku*. Tokyo: Kōdansha, 1969.

———. *Haha no kage*. Tokyo: Shinchōsha, 1994.

———. "Jicho o kataru: *Kaitō Jibago no fukkatsu*." *NEXT* 7, no. 3 (1990): 246–247.

———. *Kita Morio zenshū*. 15 vols. Tokyo: Shinchōsha, 1976–1977.

———. *Manbō no asa to Mabuze no yoru*. Tokyo: Asahi Shinbunsha, 1986.

———. *Manbō yuigonjō*. Tokyo: Shinchōsha, 2001.

———. *Seinen Mokichi: "Shakkō" "Aratama" jidai*. Tokyo: Iwanami Shoten, 2001.

———. "Senchō." In *Makkurake no ke*, 7–17. Tokyo: Shinchōsha, 1985.

———. "Sōsaku yowa." In *Kita Morio zenshū geppō*, no. 9:1–3; no. 14:1–4; no. 15:1–4. In vols. 9, 14, and 15 of *Kita Morio zenshū*. Tokyo: Shinchōsha, 1977.

———. *The Fall of the House of Nire*. Translated by Dennis Keene. New York: Kōdansha International, 1985. Originally published as *Nireke no hitobito* (Tokyo: Shinchōsha, 1964).

———. *The House of Nire*. Translated by Dennis Keene. New York: Kōdansha International, 1984. Originally published as *Nireke no hitobito* (Tokyo: Shinchōsha, 1964).

———. *Tsuki to jussento*. Tokyo: Asahi Shinbunsha, 1971.

———. "Yukiyama de tōshi." *Bungei Shunjū* (January 2005): 311–312.

——— and Saitō Yuka. *Papa wa tanoshii sōutsu-byō*. Tokyo: Shinchōsha, 2014.

"'Kunshō hoshii' to kigyō, gyōkai ga honsō." *Asahi Shinbun* (evening edition), November 8, 1986.

Mishima Yukio. "'Nireke no hitobito'." In *Ketteiban Mishima Yukio zenshū*, 33: 35. Tokyo: Shinchōsha, 2003.

Miyawaki Shunzō. *Tabi wa jiyū seki*. Tokyo: Shinchōsha, 1995.

Nada Inada. "Kaisetsu." In *Kita Morio shū*, 692–703. Vol. 61 of *Shinchō Nihon bungaku*. Tokyo: Shinchōsha, 1968.

———. "Kita Morio to sōutsu-byō." In *Tsuitō sōtokushū Kita Morio: Dokutoru Manbō bungakukan*, 56–61. Tokyo: Kawade Shobō Shinsha.

———. "Manbō, Nihonjin o kaihō, sōutsu-byō ni hikari, Kita Morio san o itamu." *Asahi Shinbun*, October 31, 2011.

Nakamura Mitsuo. "Warai no sōshitsu." In *Nakamura Mitsuo zenshū*, 10:107–143. Tokyo: Chikuma Shobō, 1972.

Oda Shōkichi. "Warau mono to warawareru mono." In *Koten, Setsuwa hen*, 415–419. Vol. 2 of *Nihon no yūmoa*. Tokyo: Chikuma Shobō, 1987.

Okuno Takeo. *Kita Morio no bungaku sekai*. Tokyo: Chūō Kōronsha, 1978.

Orbaugh, Sharalyn. "Naturalism and the Emergence of the *Shishōsetsu* (Personal Novel)." In *The Columbia Companion to Modern East Asian Literature*, edited by Joshua S. Mostow, Kirk A. Denton, Bruce Fulton, and Sharalyn Orbaugh, 137–140. New York: Columbia University Press, 2003.

Peterson, Reed M. "*An Account of My Perplexities: The Humorous Essays of Kita Morio*." PhD diss., University of Arizona, 2009.

Rimer, J. Thomas, and Van C. Gessel, eds. *The Columbia Anthology of Modern Japanese Literature.* 2 vols. New York: Columbia University Press, 2007.

Saitō Shigeta. *Mokichi no taishū.* Tokyo: Iwanami Shoten, 2000.

Saitō Yuka. *Madogiwa OL tohoho na asa, ufufu no yoru.* Tokyo: Shinchōsha, 2006.

———. *Mōjo to yobareta shukujo: sobo Saitō Teruko no ikikata.* Tokyo: Shinchōsha, 2008.

"Shijō to yūmoa jizai: sakka Kita Morio san shikyo." *Asahi Shinbun* (evening edition), October 26, 2011.

Shinoda Hajime. "Hito to bungaku." In *Kita Morio, Tsuji Kunio shū*, by Kita Morio and Tsuji Kunio, 517–534. Vol. 87 of *Chikuma gendai bungaku taikei.* Tokyo: Chikuma Shobō, 1976.

"Shunjū." *Nihon Keizai Shinbun*, October 27, 2011.

Stretcher, Matthew C. "Purely Mass or Massively Pure? The Division Between 'Pure' and 'Mass' Literature." *Monumenta Nipponica* 51 (1996): 357–374.

Suzuki, Tomi. *Narrativing the Self: Fictions of Japanese Modernity.* Stanford: Stanford University Press, 1996.

"Tensei jingo." *Asahi Shinbun*, October 27, 2011.

Tyler, William J. "Part One: Anti-Naturalism." In *Modanizumu: Modernist Fiction from Japan 1913-1938*, edited by William Tyler, 51–167. Honolulu: University of Hawai'i Press, 2008.

Yamada Hiromitsu. "Kita Morio." In *Shin kenkyū shiryō gendai Nihon bungaku*, edited by Asai Kiyoshi, et al., 2:159–168. Tokyo: Meiji Shoin, 2000.

Yamanaka Yasuhiro. "Kita Morio no dōwa sekai to sono himitsu." *Risō* (September 1980): 45–58.

Yanagita Kunio. "Gesakusha no dentō." In *Teihon Yanagita Kunio shū*, 7:186–195. Tokyo: Chikuma Shobō.

"Yoroku." *Mainichi Shinbun*, October 27, 2011.

Yoshiyuki Junnosuke. *Machikado no tabakoya made no tabi.* Tokyo: Kōdansha, 1979.

"Yūkan madamu 'dansu hōru jiken' to bundan jin tobaku issei kenkyo." *Shinchō* (July 2005): 68–69.

"Yūmoa eien ni." *Mainichi Shinbun* (evening edition), October 26, 2011,

"Yūmoa tsuranuita isshō." *Yomiuri Shinbun* (evening edition), October 26, 2011.

TITLES IN THE NEW JAPANESE HORIZON SERIES

Indian Summer by Kanai Mieko, translated with introduction by Tomoko Aoyama and Barbara Hartley

Single Sickness and Other Stories by Misuda Mizuko, translated with introduction by Lynne Kutsukake

The Art of Being Alone: Tanikawa Shuntarō Poems 1952–2009, translated with introduction by Takako U. Lento

Of Birds Crying by Minako Ōba, translated with introduction by Michiko N. Wilson and Michael K. Wilson

Red Ghost, White Ghost: Stories and Essays by Kita Morio, translated with introduction by Masako Inamoto

Pioneers of Modern Japanese Poetry, translated with introduction by Takako Lento

The Wasteland (Arano) by Takako Takahashi, translated with introduction by Britten Dean

CORNELL EAST ASIA SERIES

4 Fredrick Teiwes, *Provincial Leadership in China: The Cultural Revolution and Its Aftermath*
8 Cornelius C. Kubler, *Vocabulary and Notes to Ba Jin's Jia: An Aid for Reading the Novel*
16 Monica Bethe & Karen Brazell, *Nō as Performance: An Analysis of the Kuse Scene of Yamamba.* Available for purchase: DVD by Monica Bethe & Karen Brazell, "Yamanba: The Old Woman of the Mountains"
18 Royall Tyler, tr., *Granny Mountains: A Second Cycle of Nō Plays*
23 Knight Biggerstaff, *Nanking Letters, 1949*
28 Diane E. Perushek, ed., *The Griffis Collection of Japanese Books: An Annotated Bibliography*
37 J. Victor Koschmann, Ōiwa Keibō & Yamashita Shinji, eds., *International Perspectives on Yanagita Kunio and Japanese Folklore Studies*
38 James O'Brien, tr., *Murō Saisei: Three Works*
40 Kubo Sakae, *Land of Volcanic Ash: A Play in Two Parts,* revised edition, tr. David G. Goodman
44 Susan Orpett Long, *Family Change and the Life Course in Japan*
48 Helen Craig McCullough, *Bungo Manual: Selected Reference Materials for Students of Classical Japanese*
49 Susan Blakeley Klein, *Ankoku Butō: The Premodern and Postmodern Influences on the Dance of Utter Darkness*
50 Karen Brazell, ed., *Twelve Plays of the Noh and Kyōgen Theaters*
51 David G. Goodman, ed., *Five Plays by Kishida Kunio*
52 Shirō Hara, *Ode to Stone,* tr. James Morita
53 Peter J. Katzenstein & Yutaka Tsujinaka, *Defending the Japanese State: Structures, Norms and the Political Responses to Terrorism and Violent Social Protest in the 1970s and 1980s*
54 Su Xiaokang & Wang Luxiang, *Deathsong of the River: A Reader's Guide to the Chinese TV Series* Heshang, trs. Richard Bodman & Pin P. Wan
55 Jingyuan Zhang, *Psychoanalysis in China: Literary Transformations, 1919–1949*
56 Jane Kate Leonard & John R. Watt, eds., *To Achieve Security and Wealth: The Qing Imperial State and the Economy, 1644–1911*
57 Andrew F. Jones, *Like a Knife: Ideology and Genre in Contemporary Chinese Popular Music*
58 Peter J. Katzenstein & Nobuo Okawara, *Japan's National Security: Structures, Norms and Policy Responses in a Changing World*
59 Carsten Holz, *The Role of Central Banking in China's Economic Reforms*
60 Chifumi Shimazaki, *Warrior Ghost Plays from the Japanese Noh Theater: Parallel Translations with Running Commentary*
61 Emily Groszos Ooms, *Women and Millenarian Protest in Meiji Japan: Deguchi Nao and Ōmotokyō*
62 Carolyn Anne Morley, *Transformation, Miracles, and Mischief: The Mountain Priest Plays of Kyōgen*
63 David R. McCann & Hyunjae Yee Sallee, tr., *Selected Poems of Kim Namjo,* afterword by Kim Yunsik

64 Hua Qingzhao, *From Yalta to Panmunjom: Truman's Diplomacy and the Four Powers, 1945-1953*
65 Margaret Benton Fukasawa, *Kitahara Hakushū: His Life and Poetry*
66 Kam Louie, ed., *Strange Tales from Strange Lands: Stories by Zheng Wanlong*
67 Wang Wen-hsing, *Backed Against the Sea*, tr. Edward Gunn
69 Brian Myers, *Han Sōrya and North Korean Literature: The Failure of Socialist Realism in the DPRK*
70 Thomas P. Lyons & Victor Nee, eds., *The Economic Transformation of South China: Reform and Development in the Post-Mao Era*
71 David G. Goodman, tr., *After Apocalypse: Four Japanese Plays of Hiroshima and Nagasaki,* with introduction
72 Thomas Lyons, *Poverty and Growth in a South China County: Anxi, Fujian, 1949–1992*
74 Martyn Atkins, *Informal Empire in Crisis: British Diplomacy and the Chinese Customs Succession, 1927-1929*
76 Chifumi Shimazaki, *Restless Spirits from Japanese Noh Plays of the Fourth Group: Parallel Translations with Running Commentary*
77 Brother Anthony of Taizé & Young-Moo Kim, trs., *Back to Heaven: Selected Poems of Ch'ŏn Sang Pyŏng*
78 Kevin O'Rourke, tr., *Singing Like a Cricket, Hooting Like an Owl: Selected Poems by Yi Kyu-bo*
79 Irit Averbuch, *The Gods Come Dancing: A Study of the Japanese Ritual Dance of Yamabushi Kagura*
80 Mark Peterson, *Korean Adoption and Inheritance: Case Studies in the Creation of a Classic Confucian Society*
81 Yenna Wu, tr., *The Lioness Roars: Shrew Stories from Late Imperial China*
82 Thomas Lyons, *The Economic Geography of Fujian: A Sourcebook*, Vol. 1
83 Pak Wan-so, *The Naked Tree*, tr. Yu Young-nan
84 C.T. Hsia, *The Classic Chinese Novel: A Critical Introduction*
85 Cho Chong-Rae, *Playing With Fire*, tr. Chun Kyung-Ja
86 Hayashi Fumiko, *I Saw a Pale Horse and Selections from Diary of a Vagabond*, tr. Janice Brown
87 Motoori Norinaga, *Kojiki-den, Book 1*, tr. Ann Wehmeyer
88 Chang Soo Ko, tr., *Sending the Ship Out to the Stars: Poems of Park Je-chun*
89 Thomas Lyons, *The Economic Geography of Fujian: A Sourcebook*, Vol. 2
90 Brother Anthony of Taizé, tr., Midang: *Early Lyrics of So Chong-Ju*
92 Janice Matsumura, *More Than a Momentary Nightmare: The Yokohama Incident and Wartime Japan*
93 Kim Jong-Gil tr., *The Snow Falling on Chagall's Village: Selected Poems of Kim Ch'un-Su*
94 Wolhee Choe & Peter Fusco, trs., *Day-Shine: Poetry by Hyon-jong Chong*
95 Chifumi Shimazaki, *Troubled Souls from Japanese Noh Plays of the Fourth Group*
96 Hagiwara Sakutarō, *Principles of Poetry (Shi no Genri)*, tr. Chester Wang
97 Mae J. Smethurst, *Dramatic Representations of Filial Piety: Five Noh in Translation*
99 William Wilson, *Hōgen Monogatari: Tale of the Disorder in Hōgen*
100 Yasushi Yamanouchi, J. Victor Koschmann and Ryūichi Narita, eds., *Total War and 'Modernization'*
101 Yi Ch'ŏng-jun, *The Prophet and Other Stories*, tr. Julie Pickering
102 S.A. Thornton, *Charisma and Community Formation in Medieval Japan: The Case of the Yugyō-ha (1300-1700)*

103 Sherman Cochran, ed., *Inventing Nanjing Road: Commercial Culture in Shanghai, 1900-1945*
104 Harold M. Tanner, *Strike Hard! Anti-Crime Campaigns and Chinese Criminal Justice, 1979-1985*
105 Brother Anthony of Taizé & Young-Moo Kim, trs., *Farmers' Dance: Poems by Shin Kyŏng-nim*
106 Susan Orpett Long, ed., *Lives in Motion: Composing Circles of Self and Community in Japan*
107 Peter J. Katzenstein, Natasha Hamilton-Hart, Kozo Kato, & Ming Yue, *Asian Regionalism*
108 Kenneth Alan Grossberg, *Japan's Renaissance: The Politics of the Muromachi Bakufu*
109 John W. Hall & Toyoda Takeshi, eds., *Japan in the Muromachi Age*
110 Kim Su-Young, Shin Kyong-Nim, Lee Si-Young; *Variations: Three Korean Poets;* trs. Brother Anthony of Taizé & Young-Moo Kim
111 Samuel Leiter, *Frozen Moments: Writings on* Kabuki, *1966–2001*
118 Mae J. Smethurst and Christina Laffin, eds., *The Noh* Ominameshi*: A Flower Viewed from Many Directions*
112 Pilwun Shih Wang & Sarah Wang, *Early One Spring: A Learning Guide to Accompany the Film Video* February
113 Thomas Conlan, *In Little Need of Divine Intervention: Scrolls of the Mongol Invasions of Japan*
114 Jane Kate Leonard & Robert Antony, eds., *Dragons, Tigers, and Dogs: Qing Crisis Management and the Boundaries of State Power in Late Imperial China*
115 Shu-ning Sciban & Fred Edwards, eds., *Dragonflies: Fiction by Chinese Women in the Twentieth Century*
116 David G. Goodman, ed., *The Return of the Gods: Japanese Drama and Culture in the 1960s*
117 Yang Hi Choe-Wall, *Vision of a Phoenix: The Poems of Hŏ Nansŏrhŏn*
119 Joseph A. Murphy, *Metaphorical Circuit: Negotiations Between Literature and Science in Twentieth-Century Japan*
120 Richard F. Calichman, *Takeuchi Yoshimi: Displacing the West*
121 Fan Pen Li Chen, *Visions for the Masses: Chinese Shadow Plays from Shaanxi and Shanxi*
122 S. Yumiko Hulvey, *Sacred Rites in Moonlight: Ben no Naishi Nikki*
123 Tetsuo Najita and J. Victor Koschmann, *Conflict in Modern Japanese History: The Neglected Tradition*
124 Naoki Sakai, Brett de Bary, & Iyotani Toshio, eds., *Deconstructing Nationality*
125 Judith N. Rabinovitch and Timothy R. Bradstock, *Dance of the Butterflies: Chinese Poetry from the Japanese Court Tradition*
126 Yang Gui-ja, *Contradictions*, trs. Stephen Epstein and Kim Mi-Young
127 Ann Sung-hi Lee, *Yi Kwang-su and Modern Korean Literature:* Mujŏng
128 Pang Kie-chung & Michael D. Shin, eds., *Landlords, Peasants, & Intellectuals in Modern Korea*
129 Joan R. Piggott, ed., *Capital and Countryside in Japan, 300–1180: Japanese Historians Interpreted in English*
130 Kyoko Selden and Jolisa Gracewood, eds., *Annotated Japanese Literary Gems: Stories by Tawada Yōko, Nakagami Kenji, and Hayashi Kyōko* (Vol. 1)
131 Michael G. Murdock, *Disarming the Allies of Imperialism: The State, Agitation, and Manipulation during China's Nationalist Revolution, 1922–1929*
132 Noel J. Pinnington, *Traces in the Way: Michi and the Writings of Komparu Zenchiku*

133 Charlotte von Verschuer, *Across the Perilous Sea: Japanese Trade with China and Korea from the Seventh to the Sixteenth Centuries*, tr. Kristen Lee Hunter
134 John Timothy Wixted, *A Handbook to Classical Japanese*
135 Kyoko Selden and Jolisa Gracewoord, with Lili Selden, eds., *Annotated Japanese Literary Gems: Stories by Natsume Sōseki, Tomioka Taeko, and Inoue Yasushi* (Vol. 2)
136 Yi Tae-Jin, *The Dynamics of Confucianism and Modernization in Korean History*
137 Jennifer Rudolph, *Negotiated Power in Late Imperial China: The Zongli Yamen and the Politics of Reform*
138 Thomas D. Loooser, *Visioning Eternity: Aesthetics, Politics, and History in the Early Modern Noh Theater*
139 Gustav Heldt, *The Pursuit of Harmony: Poetry and Power in Late Heian Japan*
140 Joan R. Piggott and Yoshida Sanae, *Teishinkōki: The Year 939 in the Journal of Regent Fujiwara no Tadahira*
141 Robert Bagley, *Max Loehr and the Study of Chinese Bronzes: Style and Classification in the History of Art*
142 Edwin A. Cranston, *The Secret Island and the Enticing Flame: Worlds of Memory, Discovery, and Loss in Japanese Poetry*
143 Hugh de Ferranti, *The Last Biwa Singer: A Blind Musician in History, Imagination and Performance*
144 Roger des Forges, Minglu Gao, Liu Chiao-mei, Haun Saussy, with Thomas Burkman, eds., *Chinese Walls in Time and Space: A Multidisciplinary Perspective*
145 Hye-jin Juhn Sidney & George Sidney, trs., *I Heard Life Calling Me: Poems of Yi Sŏng-bok*
146 Sherman Cochran & Paul G. Pickowicz, eds., *China on the Margins*
147 Wang Lingzhen & Mary Ann O' Donnell, trs., *Years of Sadness: Autobiographical Writings of Wang Anyi*
148 John Holstein, tr., *A Moment's Grace: Stories from Korea in Transition*
149 Sunyoung Park in collaboration with Jefferson J.A. Gatrall, trs., *On the Eve of the Uprising and Other Stories from Colonial Korea*
150 Brother Anthony of Taizé & Lee Hyung-jin, trs., *Walking on a Washing Line: Poems of Kim Seung-Hee*
151 Matthew Fraleigh, trs., with introduction, *New Chronicles of Yanagibashi and Diary of a Journey to the West: Narushima Ryūhoku Reports from Home and Abroad*
152 Pei Huang, *Reorienting the Manchus: A Study of Sinicization, 1583–1795*
153 Karen Gernant & Chen Zeping, *White Poppies and Other Stories by Zhang Kangkang*
154 Mattias Burell & Marina Svensson, eds., *Making Law Work: Chinese Laws in Context*
155 Tomoko Aoyama & Barbara Hartley, trs., *Indian Summer by Kanai Mieko*
156 Lynne Kutsukake, tr., *Single Sickness and Other Stories by Masuda Mizuko*
157 Takako U. Lento, tr. with introduction, *Tanikawa Shuntarō: The Art of Being Alone, Poems 1952–2009*
158 Shu-ning Sciban & Fred Edwards, eds., *Endless War: Fiction & Essays by Wang Wen-hsing*
159 Elizabeth Oyler & Michael Watson, eds., *Like Clouds and Mists: Studies and Translations of Nō Plays of the Genpei War*
160 Michiko N. Wilson & Michael K. Wilson, trs., *Of Birds Crying by Minako Ōba*
161 Chifumi Shimazaki & Stephen Comee *Supernatural Beings from Japanese Noh Plays of the Fifth Group: Parallel Translations with Running Commentary*
162 Petrus Liu, *Stateless Subjects: Chinese Martial Arts Literature and Postcolonial History*
163 Lim Beng Choo, *Another Stage: Kanze Nobumitsu and the Late Muromachi Noh Theater*

164 Scott Cook, *The Bamboo Texts of Guodian: A Study and Complete Translation, Volume 1*
165 Scott Cook, *The Bamboo Texts of Guodian: A Study and Complete Translation, Volume 2*
166 Stephen D. Miller, translations with Patrick Donnelly, *The Wind from Vulture Peak: The Buddhification of Japanese Waka in the Heian Period*
167 Theodore Hughes, Jae-yong Kim, Jin-kyung Lee & Sang-kyung Lee, eds., *Rat Fire: Korean Stories from the Japanese Empire*
168 Ken C. Kawashima, Fabian Schäfer, Robert Stolz, eds., *Tosaka Jun: A Critical Reader*
169 John R. Bentley, *Tamakatsuma—A Window into the Scholarship of Motoori Norinaga*
170 Dandan Zhu, *1956: Mao's China and the Hungarian Crisis*
172 Sherman Cochran, ed., *The Capitalist Dilemma in China's Cultural Revolution*
173 Eunju Kim, tr., *Portrait of a Suburbanite: Poems of Ch'oe Seung-ja*
174 Christina Laffin, Joan Piggott & Yoshida Sanae, eds., *The Birth of a Monarch 1103: Selections from Fujiwara no Munetada's Journal* Chūyūki
175 J. Marshall Unger, Sangaku *Proofs: A Japanese Mathematician at Work*
176 Naomi Fukumori, *In Spring the Dawn: Sei Shōnagon's Makura no sōshi (The Pillow Book) and the Poetics of Amusement*
177 John B. Weinstein, *Voices of Taiwanese Women: Three Contemporary Plays*
178 Shu-ning Sciban & Ihor Pidhainy, eds., *Reading Wang Wenxing: Critical Essays*
179 Hou Xiaojia, *Negotiating Socialism in Rural China: Mao, Peasants, and Local Cadres in Shanxi, 1949–1953*
180 Joseph Esherick & Matthew Combs, eds., *1943: China at the Crossroads*
181 Rebecca Jennison & Brett de Bary, eds., *Still Hear The Wound: Toward an Asia, Politics, and Art to Come*
182 Nicholas Morrow Williams, *The Residue of Dreams: Selected Poems of Jao Tsung-i*
183 Bishop D. McKendree, *Barbed Wire and Rice: Poems and Songs from Japanese Prisoner-of-War Camps*
184 John R. Bentley, An Anthology of Kokugaku Scholars, 1690 to 1898
185 Elizabeth Markham, Naoko Terauchi, Rembrandt Wolpert, eds., *What the Doctor Overheard: Dr. Leopold Müller's Account of Music in Early Meiji Japan. Einige Notizen über die japanische Musik.* 日本音楽に関するノート *(1874–1876)*
186 Glynne Walley, *Edification, Entertainment, and Kyokutei Bakin's* Nansō Satomi hakkenden
187 Yung-Hee Kim, *Gendered Landscapes: Short Fiction by Modern and Contemporary Korean Women Novelists*
188 Masako Inamoto, *Red Ghost, White Ghost: Stories and Essays by Kita Morio*
189 J. Marshall Unger, Sangaku *Reflections: A Japanese Mathematician Teaches*
190 Jeff E. Long, *Stories from the Samurai Fringe: Hayashi Fusao's Proletarian Short Stories and the Turn to Ultranationalism in Early Shōwa Japan*
191 Ihor Pidhainy, Roger Des Forges, Grace S. Fong, *Representing Lives in China: Forms of Biography in the Ming-Qing Period*
192 Michael Pettid, ed., *Silvery World and Other Stories. Anthology of Korean Literature Vol. 1*

eap.einaudi.cornell.edu/publications